CAUGHT STEALING

Caught Stealing

Steve Trout

DEDICATION

This book is dedicated to a very special friend.

In 1990 the IRS sent me a note saying I owed an enormous amount of money. The next four years were terribly frustrating and costly in trying to find experts to help settle the debt. Then I met a special person in a charity golf outing who offered to help. He suggested I bring the financial information and prospectuses of my investments to his accounting office.

Slowly he found mistakes in tax deductions, mismanagement of investments, and other financial red flags.
Over the next ten years of IRS meetings, payments to the debt and a clear view of the investments, I saw light at the end of the tunnel.

This kind and empathetic man was a savior to me. I'm happy to say we are still good friends.

Caught Stealing
Baseball's Wild Wild West Years

A NOVEL BY STEVE TROUT

ISBN: 979-8-89282-205-3
© Copyright 2025
All Rights Reserved
Printed in the United States of America

Rainbow Trout Books

PROLOGUE

I am a former major league pitcher who pitched for 11 years in the big leagues. In my first book, *"Home Plate,"* I described my own baseball career, including being drafted out of high school into the minor leagues, the highlights as one of the few pitchers who pitched successfully for both the Chicago White Sox and the Chicago Cubs, and the later disappointments with the New York Yankees and the Seattle Mariners after I inexplicably lost my baseball "radar."

I also chronicled the 15-year major league career of my father, Paul "Dizzy" Trout. Our combined careers resulted in 258 major league wins, the second-highest number of wins by any father-son tandem ever to pitch in the major leagues.

My primary purpose in writing *"Home Plate"* was to give fans and readers an idea of what it was like for my dad and me to pitch in the major leagues throughout our careers, and also what it was like to grow up in a large family as my dad continued with a career in baseball as an executive in the front office.

What I did not do in *"**Home Plate,**"* but will do in this book, is inform both baseball fans and readers about a different side of baseball through the years – the seamy, avaricious nature of baseball agents and their treatment (or mistreatment) of their baseball player clients throughout their baseball careers and their post-career aftermath.

It is this dark underbelly of baseball representation that should be exposed and understood, so that fans and readers alike can understand why there have been so many stories appearing in the media about baseball players who have ended up poor, destitute or bankrupt in spite of the millions of dollars they earned during the course of their careers.

During my dad's career and for many years thereafter, most baseball players were not paid enough to allow them to relax during their off-season. Instead, especially if they had to support families, they were forced to work during the off-season to pay their year-round bills and make ends meet. Not surprisingly, players did not have agents during those decades, because baseball was not the billion-dollar business that it is today, and players were not paid enough money to interest an agent.

All of that changed in baseball (as in other sports) with the advent of free agency and the huge increases in players' salaries. Owners got into bidding wars to attract and sign good players and relatively trusting players were wooed by smooth-talking "businessmen," who represented themselves as "agents."

These agents claimed they had unique "experience" to land the biggest contract for the player, and the "expertise" to help the player invest the forthcoming big dollars, so they could maximize future income for the rest of their life. They falsely claimed all they wanted from the player was just a percentage of the player's contract amount. This "agent business" quickly expanded throughout the major leagues, with little or no regulation, either by major league baseball or by the baseball players association.

As a former major leaguer, I believe what baseball fans have never seen are the off-the-field experiences of the players dealing with baseball "agents" during their major league careers, and after their playing days. I was just out of high school with no background in how this nasty business operated. Neither my siblings, nor my pitcher father, could ever comprehend what was behind the curtain of the new, often corrupt world of agents. These businessmen, many with law degrees, were happy to jump on the highway of big money being made by unsuspecting baseball players.

The most turbulent baseball agent period was the early free agency "The Wild-Wild West" years, beginning after the late 1975 Messersmith-McNally arbitration decision that opened the "free agency" flood gates, and continuing through at least the 1988 initial adoption of the Major League Baseball Players Association's Regulations Governing Players Agents. This was when both American and foreign baseball players became the targets of unscrupulous characters who crawled out of the woodwork and claimed to be "agents."

It was during this period that I was drafted in 1976, began my major league years in 1978, and after my career in 1989. I am surviving proof, as are many players like me, of the severe loss of hundreds of thousands of dollars (if not millions) as a result of the trust I had in my agents.

I know what it was like to see the money disappear with little or no return and only nebulous explanations as to why. I know what it was like to be informed of the existence of large tax bills by the IRS and the lack of investment income to pay those bills.

I know what it was like to experience "rock bottom," performing maintenance activities and helping fold towels at a Holiday Inn, while punching a time clock making only minimum wage. I know what it was like to discover the misdeeds of agents years later and the difficulty of trying to recover any of my evaporated funds. I know what it has been like to rebuild my life after all of these "roller coaster" experiences.

The plethora of player/agent conflicts of financial interest and fiduciary neglect finally set off the alarm that something had to be done to protect the players from the crooked lawyers and other advisors. However, since it took over ten years to regulate the agents, the harm had already been done. Once-wealthy players were discovering great losses and personal horrors caused by those who cheated them out of millions.

I have written this book as autobiographical fiction. All characters in this book are fictional, but their experiences are, tragically, all too real.

Steve Trout

1

Clarksville, Illinois was not a booming metropolis – it wasn't even *close* to any metropolis. It was a small town located in Shelby County in central Illinois, right in the middle of a rural area that contained extremely rich soil, making it one of the most productive corn and soybean growing areas not only in Illinois but in the entire Midwest.

Many of the Clarksville area farms had been operated by the same families for generations. The residents of both the town and surrounding area were close-knit, proud of their farms, their families, and their community. Clarksville's children and schools were a major focal point throughout the entire school year, especially their teenagers in Clarksville High School sports. The healthy regimen of farm activities seemed to result in their kids growing stronger by the month.

They frequently fielded competitive teams in all their major sports, but 1976 was a special year for the baseball team, especially for two of its seniors, Glenn Chance and Ross Borgia. They were the team's star shortstop and pitcher, respectively, who led the team to its first ever high school state championship. They had strong but different personalities, with the consensus being that they both had very bright futures.

Glenn Chance's high school years were loaded with memories and highlights, but the most important one to him, even more than the state championship, was his relationship with Lisa Connors, the popular blonde who became his high school sweetheart. Lisa was the heart throb of many guys, some jocks, some long hairs. However it was Glenn who stole her heart. Lisa was no easy date; it was Glenn's tenacity that finally got her to say yes to a Friday night movie.

Baseball didn't have cheerleaders, but girls flocked to the baseball field wearing jeans with warm coats, as baseball could get very cold in the Spring. Lisa stirred up the interest among the girls in going to baseball games, doing it first to support Glenn, but then realizing she really enjoyed baseball.

Lisa reminded the girls that many of the guys on the baseball team also played other sports. Lisa never missed a game; she was falling for Glenn just like he was for her. Lisa strongly believed that their puppy love would turn into true love. Glenn's teammate Ross Borgia was their ace pitcher, a 6'2" crew-cut left-hander with a live fastball, effective control, plus some pop in his bat.

They were the talk of both the town and professional scouts. They bonded under the reality of being pro material. They were as different as a hammer is to a shovel, but baseball has only one language. Glenn was more of a hippie, a free spirit; he marched to the beat of a different drummer. He liked concerts, shooting pool, and doing landscape jobs during non-baseball days in the summer.

In high school Ross focused on his studies and his pitching. During his third year on the varsity team, Ross piled up some impressive numbers. He knew in order to be great, you had to be very focused, determined and dedicated to the degree that you made an all-in commitment.

In a scout's opinion, the best players developed a mastery of their sport, and in baseball it included studying how infielders moved, how outfielders tracked line drives hit right at them, the weight of the bat, how a batter conducted his preparation in the batter's box.

In school, Ross was shy. Going out with a group was okay, but one-on-one was a different matter. Ross would always say, "be ready for the what ifs." What if you got hurt, what if your parents died, what if you got a girl pregnant? He thought about such things.

On June 8th everything changed for both of them. Phone calls came into each home, one from the Minnesota Twins and one from the Atlanta Braves. Glenn was selected as the tenth pick in the second round by the Twins. Glenn sat and smiled, thinking about how he would ask Lisa to marry him after signing a $90,000.00 bonus.

He custom made a jersey for her that read MRS. CHANCE. Lisa didn't hesitate to say yes; she threw out the idea of attending college, replacing her independence to be the wife of a ball player. Glenn signed his contract with the Twins on the second day after the draft. Glenn's father advised him to sign it before they might take it off the table.

Glenn thought, "Why try to negotiate a bigger bonus? Let's not get off on the wrong foot as a pro player."

Ross was a fourth-round draft pick by the Atlanta Braves. He received a $45,000.00 bonus from the Braves, which was almost double what a routine fourth round pick might receive, but Ross was able to leverage a college scholarship offered by the University of Illinois into getting the higher bonus.

The more leverage that you've got against a team, the more money you can get. Ross put the money into a three-year CD, gaining a better rate of interest than by just putting it into a savings account. He didn't feel rich, but he felt that it would tide him over for three years in the minor leagues, enough time for him to find out if he was good enough to be a big leaguer.

2

Pro ball was an eye opener; everyone was good, guys were big and strong with many Latinos. This can be very intimidating to rookies, now having to compete against guys coming from top colleges and others that arrive from the Dominican Republic, Venezuela and other countries.

Glenn's first assignment in the minor leagues was to the Twins' Class A Rookie ball, the Elizabethton Twins in Elizabethton, Tennessee in the Appalachian League. Even though it was only going to be for a couple summer months, Glenn was looking forward to finding out what pro ball was like.

He found out that he loved the short season, hitting well and fielding well. He thought that hitting in pro ball was easier than hitting in high school, telling Lisa that, although the pitchers are good, they throw the ball closer to the plate most of the time. He explained that it's easier to prepare mentally to hit if you know the ball will be in a location where you can hit it.

Glenn hired his agent, Allen Sharpe, during the second week of the short rookie season. The very first thing that Sharpe did was to invest $40,000.00 of Glenn's bonus money, promising they should get a 15% return on their investments. Sharpe stated that he was putting the money into real estate buildings he was developing.

Glenn was unconcerned, since many guys had agents, and two of his minor league teammates were also represented by Sharpe. Lisa took this initial investment with a grain of salt, not wanting to upset her fiancé, although she would have preferred that the money sit in the bank.

Ross adjusted well to his short season. He was assigned to the Braves' Class A Rookie team, the Kingsport Braves in Kingsport, Tennessee, also in the Appalachian League. He was quickly exposed to a new type of training. Pro ball had a different way of teaching with towel drills, learning a cutter and how a pro batter can turn around a straight 93 mph fastball.

The first hurdle was to make his straight fastball have some movement. The pitching coach stressed that in high school a straight 93 mph fastball can be too much for hitters, but in the pros, it looks like a watermelon. Working on getting the ball to have some late movement would be ideal. Sacrificing speed for movement. Developing a change-up was the key to his future. Most high school kids fall in love with the curve ball, but in the pros, it's all about the change-up, a pitch that looks like a fastball, but is much slower and drops at the end.

Ross kept in touch with Glenn during their short season. Even though they both were very competitive, they still remained friends. In the minors you at times cross paths with those you played with in school, but being a pro is a serious matter.

During a weekend series where Glenn's Twins team was visiting Ross' Braves team in Kingsport, Glenn tried to convince Ross to meet his just-hired agent. Glenn praised Sharpe, boasting that "he just doesn't sign anybody, getting an agent shows that you've got big league potential." Ross just nodded and told Glenn, "When I'm good enough, I will get that agent and that agent will be me. I want to repre-sent myself."

When Ross went to play Glenn at Joe O'Brien Field in Elizabethton, he was on the mound and they faced each other for the first time in real competition. Ross developed a good change up from his new pitching coach striking out Glenn on the off-speed pitch. As he walked back to the dugout, Glenn yelled to him, "You didn't have that pitch in high school!" Ross flashed a big grin and nodded. The next time they would meet would be under more pleasant sur-roundings, Glenn's wedding to Lisa in November.

The short season ended well, with Ross taking home a winter training program developed by the major league team trainer. The array of shoulder exercises, squats and core workouts became part of the Braves' organization's program for excellence. There also was a book about the history of its proud past, educating the young players about what it means to be a Brave.

Returning home to live with his parents, Ross spent most of his time in the gym working on the team's fitness program. His two days a week throwing sessions helped him fine tune his mechanics and get a better feel for the change-up and the cutter. He received the invitation to Glenn and Lisa's wedding, which brought a smile to his face when he thought how Glenn and Lisa were like two peas in a pod.

After the short season ended for Glenn, the rest of the year was all about Lisa and the wedding plans. Lisa would never forget her day in the sun with a wedding of epic pro-portions. She cried so often that many became concerned, but hers were tears of joy. She was feeling so special - she got her man with a life in baseball. However, Lisa wasn't all smiles with Sharpe sitting at the head table.

She had a strange thought that maybe Glenn should have married Sharpe. However, she was told that in baseball agents became part of the family. She tried to hook up Ross with her best friend by making sure they sat at the same table. Glenn went all out to make sure that Ross had a good time, so much so that he got up on the stage with the local band and sang "You Are the Sunshine of My Life" by Stevie Wonder. He then waved Ross to join in the singing of the next song.

The night finished with the best man, Bobby Becket, Glenn's lifelong buddy, and Glenn getting down to their skivvies on the dance floor. The group ended the night at the hotel bar firing up cigars.

Ross kidded Glenn about his strikeout on the change-up, and Glenn immediately reminded him about his next at bat, a bases clearing triple on a hanging curve ball. Ross said, "I was working on that pitch," to which Glenn replied, "Not enough!" They made a small wager on who would be the first to the big leagues. Before too much more joking around, they ended up in the small hotel bar smoking cigars that set off the smoke detector and the sprinkler system.

Everybody laughed as Lisa and Glenn headed up to their honeymoon suite. "See you in spring training" were the last words shared between the two promising rookies. Ross left the same way that he came in, alone. He thought about what Glenn said about baseball in the minors, with its lonely road trips, killing time walking around malls. They agreed on the subliminal competition with your teammates. They had talked about how people thought that the life of a ball player was so cool, being on the road playing ball. How untrue, they agreed.

Players formed into cliques, with Latinos hanging tighter than the knot on your glove, southerners in cowboy boots, northerners overusing Brut cologne and hair gel.

3

Glenn left for spring training in Orlando a married man, with a short season behind him and an organization projecting him as a prospect with a high ceiling. Spring training went by fast, with Glenn getting respect from all his teammates in the locker room. What you do on the field gets you the respect off the field.

Glenn started his first full minor league season in high Class A ball playing for the Wisconsin Rapids Twins in the Midwest League. He played well, with solid defense, also displaying a leadership mentality. He became more serious about baseball, realizing that baseball was a business. Harry Warner, his manager, was so impressed by the third month that he recommended him to take the next jump to Class AA ball. The Twins' minor league director, Roland King (a/k/a "Cards"), promoted Glenn after seeing him play in a weekend series.

There was some locker room talk about Glenn's imminent call-up, and whether it would be to AA or AAA. Glenn, being not only a gifted ball player but also a smart one, did not pay any attention to the chit-chat of who would be called up. He told his friend J.C. that once you put those thoughts in your head, you become too tight, you play to be seen, forgetting the feel of the game. The game has enough pressure, so why add more?

Following a night game in which he went 4 for 4, Glenn and his teammates were playing cards waiting out a rain delay. The trainer was giving Glenn some basic treatment. He told Glenn that in AA they had a much bigger locker room with a hot tub, which definitely helped players stay loose. Whether it was a slip of the tongue or not, Glenn sensed the call-up would be coming soon.

When the game was called and rescheduled as part of a doubleheader the next day, Glenn started putting on his street clothes. Manager Lou Coletti called him into his office, telling him, "Kid, it's been great seeing you improve every day, so pack your bags. We're sending you to our Orlando, Florida team in the Class AA Southern League. Report to Manager Joe Jones." There were a few guys still lingering around, so they opened a case of beer, toasting Glenn's call-up.

When Glenn told Lisa the great news, she was as happy as any player's wife would be who supported her husband in a game that had more ups and downs than a roller coaster. The Twins wanted Glenn in Orlando by the weekend, so they hurried to get there. They made the trip with excitement, singing to the various tunes on the radio.

Glenn was looking forward to the second part of the season. They knew a few players on the Orlando team, with Lisa having a dear friend in Jennifer, Richard Hoyt's girlfriend.

The next three months flew by for Ross with great expectations for his first full season. Just after the new year, he received a package from the Atlanta Braves. The cover letter informed him that he was being assigned to their high-Class A team, the Greenwood Braves, at Greenwood, South Carolina in the Western Carolinas League. The contract that the Braves sent him to sign and return called for a salary of only $1,000.00 a month (he was glad that he had his bonus money in the bank). He sent the contract back to the Braves by certified mail, return receipt requested and kept the receipt for proof. The minor league spring training camp was held at their major league training complex in West Palm Beach, Florida.

Ross drove to West Palm Beach, arriving early to meet his host family that the ball club arranged through its housing program. The host family was a widow, Donna, living with her elderly mother and dog. She was an avid baseball fan whose husband had run a successful printing and graphics company, which the Braves used for various projects. Living only three blocks from the complex made it easy for Ross to get to and from practice after a hard day's work.

Ross was amazed at the number of Latinos that were in the locker room, most of them coming from the Dominican Republic (D.R.). Ross wondered about how many visas the team was allowed to have, just as he wondered about some of their ages. He did respect them for the sacrifice that they made just to have a very limited chance at making it to the show. He liked the guys, even though he knew they were his competition. They seemed to be a wild group of young men who loved the small-town girls.

When spring training camp opened, there were almost 200 guys in uniform in the locker-room. It made Ross think of the butcher shop back in Clarksville. Ross laughed as he thought to himself, "Hell, they call it the 'FARM' system."

The players were just a product, a tool for the construction business of baseball. After practice Ross had noticed in the coach's locker room a huge chalk board with all the farm teams' players names listed in columns. He saw the coaches sitting in a circle in front of it drinking Budweisers. Each day names were moved around, some up, down or, at worst, erased.

Spring went well, with stiff competition among well over 80 pitchers in camp looking for jobs. The five weeks had some circus-like days, such as giving tryouts to almost anyone who showed up with a glove.

One kid from Birmingham, a tall black 20-year-old who didn't know if he wanted to pitch with his right or left arm, drew a crowd in the bullpen area with his ambidextrous ability, although neither arm was good enough. Competition makes you work harder; it can also make you become selfish, hateful, dishonest.

The high draft picks showed an entitlement confidence, while the low rounders hustled to make up for the imbalance of status. The percentage of high school first round picks that will pitch in the show is about 18%, but that number increases to 31% for college first rounders.

Starting out pitching only three innings at a time, Ross stretched to six innings per game as the team got closer to breaking camp. Ross, with his 93-mph heater would be the only lefty in the Greenwood starting rotation. The average lefty in the big leagues throws about 88 mph, while a right hander needs to hit at least 93 mph. Most fathers know that being a lefty is a quickest road to the big leagues. It's really economics 101, supply and demand. Far less lefty's than righties.

The Class A Greenwood team starting rotation could be a basketball team, with Ross being the shortest at 6'2". The Braves made provisions for the team to be transported by bus to South Carolina, since a number of the players who made the club, especially the Latino free agents, didn't have cars.

Since Ross already had his car with him in Florida, he was granted permission to drive to Greenwood. He said goodbye to his host family. He thanked Donna and her mother for all their great meals.

"See you next Spring," said Ross.

Ross drove back north to Greenwood, a town of about 20,000 people located in northwest South Carolina. In the past it had been a very important mill center in the cotton industry.

The Greenwood Braves played their games at Legion Field. The park was not new, but the home locker room was newly remodeled with luxuries that young players liked. It contained a hot tub, a lunch room, a fully carpeted locker area, and a large screen TV. Ross thought the renovation was intended to have the players fall in love with the place, wanting to come early and stay late.

The team's Friday home opener had Ross keeping the pitching chart, which meant he would be Saturday night's starter. Ross had never pitched in front of 5,000 fans, so, while keeping the chart, Ross made notes about the other team's hitters.

What created the most nerves for Ross were the two tickets he had left for Beth, a pretty waitress who had served him breakfast at a diner on his first day in Greenwood. The connection started when he ordered a second order of biscuits with gravy. That led to Ross' asking her to attend Saturday night's game.

The game went well, with Ross' box score showing 6 innings, 2 runs, 1 earned, 2 walks, 4 strikeouts and 1 hit-by-pitch. Beth waited at the player's gate while striking up a conversation with the pitching coach's wife. Ross was all smiles; he got the win and Beth was looking hot in her flowery dress.

Greenwood's starting pitching staff had 5 good arms - four of them USA-bred and one from the Dominican- but the bullpen had 5 relievers, including two from the Dominican Republic and one from Mexico. The top prospect was their Dominican shortstop from San Pedro de Marcoris, a fertile city for great shortstops.

This kid had a gun for an arm that got the ball to first base in less than 2 seconds, and his body movements were like those of a professional ballerina. Ross thought, "Thank God Glenn's not on this team."

It's a dog-eat-dog life in the minors.

Ross felt the coaches try to get them to play as a team, but each pitcher wished himself more runs per game than the other starters. It was more about "who's got a live fastball" or "can you pitch from behind in the count."

Ross found comfort with Beth, making sure he sat in her section at the diner every day, but he slowed down on the two orders of biscuits with crispy fried bacon. She went to most games, certainly the ones when Ross was on the mound.

Ross had a unique pitching coach in Greenwood named Coach Brad who used various drills and instilled being a killer on the mound into his players. One drill Ross liked the most had colored plates in various sizes to help develop focus and concentration. There were 8", 11" and 14" diameter plates, and the idea was to throw all of your pitches over the various sizes from distances that fit into the throwing system.

The pitcher throws 15 pitches over each plate, finishing the bullpen pitching to the regulation size 17" wide home plate. Coach Brad had an easy way about himself, but he was known during his playing days to knock down a batter, even if he was his brother. He instilled a killer attitude often saying once you got a guy down you never let him up.

Brad was all business. His attitude was that if the pitchers saw Brad being serious about his job, they will take their jobs seriously as well. He told the staff that pitching was a mind game. He emphasized that a good relief pitcher needed to have a short memory, while a good starter needed to have a long memory, reminding the staff that you're only as good as your next outing. The team jelled well, with Ross holding his position as the number two starter and number one with Beth.

The social highlight of their summer was the second weekend in July for South Carolina's "Festival of Discovery" in Greenwood. They went to all kinds of festivities, including the South Carolina State Championship BBQ cook-off. What a life, pitching in pro ball for a first-place team and dating a southern belle!

Ross experienced mixed emotions in late July. He wondered why Coach Brad was grinning from ear to ear. "Time to hit the road, Ross! The Braves want you in Class AA Savannah, Georgia ASAP. Good luck! I know you can do it. You've earned it." As excited as Ross was to get this great news, his heart sank when he realized he'd have to say goodbye to Beth. He invited her to visit him in Savannah, promising that he would come back to see her after the season.

Ross knew nothing about Savannah. He found out that it was a pre-Revolutionary War, old South seaport city in southeast Georgia. He remembered seeing Rhett Butler in *Gone With The Wind*, and he learned that Sherman's "March To The Sea" shown in the movie was actually his march to Savannah to capture that strategic port. He found out that the Twins also had a AA team in the Southern

League in Orlando. He thought about how cool it would be if Glenn also could get promoted to AA ball by the Twins.

Ross no sooner began to adapt to Savannah and to AA ball when he got a huge surprise. He walked onto Grayson Stadium's field before the start of a weekend series against the visiting Orlando Twins, when he heard a voice yelling behind him, "Hey, Rag Arm, what are you doing up here – they need a batting practice pitcher?"

He turned around and was amazed to see Glenn in an Orlando Twins uniform. Ross yelled back, "Nah, they told me they needed someone to shut down some hot shot shortstop in this league!" They agreed to meet Saturday night after the game.

Initially, Ross had the upper hand over Glenn in Saturday night's game. Glenn was 0 for 2 when he stepped to the plate in the seventh inning in a scoreless tie. Then, after a one out walk, Ross second baseman threw a double play ball into left field, putting runners at first and third base.

Glenn hit a sacrifice fly to right field, driving in the only run of the game. That left each of them with bragging rights at dinner – Ross held Glenn hitless, but Glenn drove in the winning run to saddle Ross with the defeat. At dinner they enjoyed comparing notes on their first full minor league season.

Ross asked Glenn how Lisa was surviving the summer in Orlando's humidity. "Swimming pools, air conditioning, and night games" was Glenn's answer. Hard work was paying off for the two Clarksville classmates! They agreed to spend some time together during the winter.

As the season continued, it became the longest one that Ross had ever pitched. The season's physical demand seemed to get more challenging on his young left arm, to the point where Ross started developing some concern.

He mentioned it to his new pitching coach, who told him that most pitchers go through a dead arm period. A pitcher's main muscles are the ones in the back of the shoulder, the rotator cuff; now Ross realized he had a real dead arm. That's when the fastball has lost a few miles per hour, and the curve ball breaks a little less sharply.

Dead arm happens to most pitchers at one time or another. Ironically, Ross still got his ground ball outs, but his strikeouts went down. There was no denying it: his arm was getting weaker. With no pop, no life on his pitches, Ross thought of shutting it down for one start.

However, the pitching coach stressed a mindset that dead arm is not an injury, you have to work through the soreness in order to make it stronger. Ross followed his advice, even though each start became more painful. The pain developed into a burning sensation in the back-shoulder area.

It was in early August, with only three starts left. Ross would never forget his 55th pitch on August 8, 1977. If dates are memories of historical events, this was the date that signaled the end of a promising baseball career.

He felt a pop and immediate pain in his left shoulder, after which he just let his arm dangle by his side. The trainer came running out, but Ross just walked right off, telling him "My arm isn't dead, it's gone!"

Their Savannah orthopedic doctor examined him in the locker room and told Ross he suspected a tear in his shoulder. Ross was devastated when he was given the initial diagnosis. The players' minor league contracts did not contain any right to medical treatment for the players, whether for major or minor injuries. However, since players were like a team's inventory, it made sense to the teams to at least protect their investment to a certain extent by using team trainers and physicians.

Nevertheless, it ultimately was the team's decision whether to provide treatment at all (and, if so, to what extent) or to provide the player with his outright release. Frequently, the better the player, the more treatment the team will provide.

However, major league clubs realized that each June draft would bring them another crop of over 30 players of their own selection, many playing the same position now or in the future that the injured player(s) currently played, especially the pitchers. The treatment decision was in the team's hands, not the player's (unless the player filed for workers' compensation in the appropriate state).

Ross was not in a good mood when asked to attend a meeting in the Savannah team office. In the room were the general manager, the team manager and the team trainer. Ross had a very dim view of the trainer, since the trainer had not disagreed with the pitching coach's dead arm theory and didn't try to protect Ross in any way.

Ross held both of them equally responsible for contributing to his rotator cuff injury. Ross did not know the fourth guy in the room, who was introduced to him as the Braves' minor league personnel director, Brad Reynolds.

Reynolds got right to the point, saying, "Ross, we want you to know how sorry we all are about your injury. We've been impressed by your progress in the last two seasons, and you definitely figured in our future plans.

"We've talked it over in Atlanta, and that's why I've driven down here to talk directly with you. After discussing your condition with our team orthopedic surgeon, we want to send you to Los Angeles for treatment and possible surgery at the Jobe-Kerlan Clinic at UCLA.

"We can't force you to undergo surgery, and there's no guarantee that it will be successful. We do think it's worth taking the chance, and we think that both you and the Braves want to do whatever is possible to see if you can come back from this injury. Do you want to give it a try?"

Ross knew what his answer was going to be as soon as Reynolds had finished. He quickly responded, "Yes, I certainly do. How will all of this work?"

Reynolds explained further that the whole process would be coordinated directly by his office. He said that an appointment already had been made with Dr. Dan Curtin at the Jobe-Kerlan Clinic at UCLA.

All of his medical treatment bills, his hotel bills and his restaurant charges would be sent directly to the Braves for their payment. When Ross was able to return to Illinois, his rehabilitation would be supervised by the orthopedic staff at the Carle Clinic in Champaign. Physical therapy could be conducted either there or at a local facility, if available.

The Carle Clinic would provide reports to both Dr. Curtin and the Braves. All travel expenses would be paid by the Braves. Finally, until a final medical decision was made one way or the other, the Braves would keep paying his current minor league salary. Reynolds gave him his business card with his office telephone number, as well as the telephone number for his assistant, June Summers, who would be his primary contact person.

Ross felt very apprehensive during his flight to Los Angeles. Leaving the team behind was a surrealistic feeling – was he in a dream, a fearful mindset of fog? No, this was harsh reality. Saying goodbye to his "BIBs" (Brothers In Baseball) had torn him apart. In order to make it through his goodbyes, he had handed letters to his special buddies.

Ross quickly felt comfortable with Dr. Curtin. He took his time examining Ross's left shoulder. He used a physical mockup of his shoulder, demonstrating not only where he thought the tear was but also showing Ross the muscles that he would have to cut through to get access to repair the tear.

He explained to Ross how many of these procedures he had performed, along with the success rate. Ross appreciated his candor. He explained the suturing process and went into detail about what Ross could expect during his rehabilitation program, both in LA and then in Illinois. Ross made his ultimate decision by the time Dr. Curtin completed his explanation.

He told him, "Let's go for it."

Ross saw Dr. Curtin just before the surgery. After it was over, Dr. Curtin told him at his bedside that the procedure went as well as possible. He explained that he had encountered some problems, which he had addressed as best he could. He said the rest of the treatment was now going to be up to Ross and how hard he was going to work during rehabilitation.

Ross was glad to finally be released from the hospital, but he was bored at his hotel during the initial weeks after surgery. One highlight that relieved his boredom was Reggie Jackson's 3-homer game for the Yankees in the World Series.

Ross saw Dr. Curtin in his office in early December. The doctor congratulated him on his progress so far, but he said there was still a lot to do. Ross agreed.

He did finally ask Dr. Curtin the question that had been bothering him for months, "If we had shut my arm down when I was experiencing the 'dead arm' condition, would my rotator cuff tear still have occurred later and to the same extent?"

Ross felt that Dr. Curtin was tap dancing around the question when he answered, "That's hard to tell. I'm not sure."

Ross knew that the evasiveness that he sensed in Dr. Curtin's answer would bother him for a long time. Ross went directly back to Clarksville, leaving everything else behind. His sole focus was going to be his rehab.

4

Glenn was invited to the big-league camp in Orlando. The Twins wanted to show him that he was on their radar. You get free gloves, baseball card companies taking pictures, and the meal money was great. There was also an off-hotel housing budget increase, so Lisa and Glenn temporarily upgraded their living situation to a small resort where a few big leaguers stayed.

This would be short-lived, since he would be only two weeks in the big-league camp. The experience was an eye-opener. Once Glenn reported back to the minor league camp, he took the locker next to his buddy, Richard Hoyt. Hoyt was also on the radar; both of them wanted the big-league life.

Joe Jones was happy to have Glenn back. He told him, "Having you around, Glenn, makes me look like I know what I'm doing." Having both spring training and the AA team in Orlando made it easier for Glenn and Lisa to pick up from where they had left off last year. Maybe it was the comfort of the place, plus the success he had enjoyed, but things just seemed right to Glenn. However, Glenn didn't want to stay there any longer than necessary, now that he tasted big league life for two weeks. Once a hound has the scent of a target, it never gives up until it gets what it's after.

It took only two months for the Twins organization to put a little pressure on Glenn, moving him up to the Class AAA Toledo Mud Hens in the International League. Management thought having Glenn face more seasoned pitchers was what was best for him to get ready for the show. Glenn's slight slump to start out was not too worrisome for manager Joe Sparks.

Sparks had been managing the Mud Hens for five years. He had seen many young players put too much pressure on themselves when first arriving.

Sparks had Glenn come out for early batting practice so Glenn could get more comfortable and hopefully into a groove. Cal thought maybe this might carry over into the game tonight. It did, with Glenn busting out of a 2-for-19 slump with a 3-for-4 night, including one bomb over the right field wall.

Glenn was inserted into the number 5 spot in the lineup, playing shortstop the next day, a move that came right from the top. Joe Sparks was told by the Twins to get him ready for a definite call-up. When Joe asked them when, he was told, "Soon."

Glenn was excited to be called into the manager's office; seeing the smile on Joe's face, it was apparent that the purpose of the meeting was to inform him of his call-up to the big leagues. Minnesota liked his range at short, but really saw Glenn as a roving utility guy with sure hands – someone with some pop in his bat, able to play just about wherever you put him.

In his first big league game, Glenn was inserted to play short for the eighth and ninth innings of a game in which Bill Marshall was pitching in relief.

Glenn immediately thought, "My first big league game and I'm playing behind a legend – I hope I don't screw up!"

His chance came in the ninth inning, throwing out the White Sox speedy left fielder, Bob "Speedy" Star. His box score read like a perfect game – one ground ball, one putout.

He never got to hit, but that was okay with him, since White Sox closer Ed Frazier was throwing gas with the score 6 to 1. A win made for a fun locker room full of music and beer, he quickly felt right at home with these big leaguers. He pinched himself as if dreaming when taking a shower with Stan Kingman and Willie Thompson.

Glenn got his post game food at the buffet table without a towel around his privates, which immediately resulted in the veterans howling at him. He quickly was informed that he had just committed a major locker room infraction that would subject him to a trial before the team's kangaroo court. He was brought the next day before the court. Its judge, fellow shortstop Roy Smalley (dressed in a wig and robe with a gavel), charged him with the blatant crime of "dick in the spread"!

Glenn had to pay his first team fine as a big leaguer. He pleaded no contest, if protesting the fine he'd owe double, $100 instead of $50.00. Glenn thought that was the end of it.

However, he was pleasantly surprised to be interviewed before the next game by the Twins radio broadcaster, Frank Rago.

Glenn thought to himself excitedly, "Wow, my first interview in the bigs."

He was lulled into a false sense of security by Frank's routine questions about his first major league game, how he went about playing shortstop, how the majors differed from the minors. Glenn promptly lost it when Rago asked him how the major league post game spread differed from the minors, as well as how the Twins clubhouse in general was different from the minors! Even Rago couldn't keep a straight face when he asked Glenn these "gotcha" questions. It got even worse when he discovered that the players had recorded the interview and were playing it on a speaker when he got back to the locker room.

Glenn enjoyed his entire fun-filled call up experience. Even if he never made it back to the bigs, he would have stories to tell his grandkids. He played in half of the 30 games remaining on the schedule, getting along with his teammates just fine. However, the third base coach, Bobby Winkles, gave Glenn a hard time after he ran through his stop sign, even though he was safe at home, making Winkles look bad. Hitting .263, with only 2 errors playing both shortstop and second base, his first year in the bigs went great.

The winter also went well. They lived with Lisa's parents, saving money for their future. The phone rang off the hook, with many people calling and congratulating Glenn on a good season. He was asked to speak at the Clarksville High School sports banquet, to visit the children's section at the hospital, and to appear at other community programs. The winter flew by faster than a Goose Gossage high and tight fastball.

5

Ross made it through the Christmas season okay, although it wasn't very joyful or productive, since he wasn't scheduled to start his rehab program at Carlyle Clinic until the first week in January. He met an orthopedic specialist named Dr. Eric Wilcox for his first appointment.

Wilcox performed a full examination, making a particular note of Ross's reduced range of motion in the shoulder area. He gave him a printout of exercises to gain more range of motion if he was going to pursue his baseball career. He recommended that Ross continue to schedule Tuesday-Thursday-Saturday physical therapy sessions at the Morantz clinic.

After he started his rehab program, Ross received a phone call from Glenn inviting him to dinner with him and Lisa. The dinner proceeded awkwardly for the three of them, since Glenn and Lisa were hesitant to probe Ross about his injury, his rehab, as well as his future.

Ross, in turn, found it painful to ask Glenn what it was like to play in the big leagues, and what he was looking forward to in his anticipated first full big-league season.

It seemed like unanswered thoughts hung over their table – Glenn was afraid to think about how that could have been him; Ross hated facing the fact that he may never get to play baseball again, certainly not in the big leagues. Glenn suggested that they get together again before he left for spring training next month. Ross agreed, knowing that it probably would never happen.

Ross diligently followed his rehab program at Morantz Clinic, as he also did in Clarksville. He arranged with a Clarksville's high school catcher to earn some extra money by catching him Monday, Wednesday and Friday evenings. However, neither Ross nor Dr. Wilcox was satisfied with his range of motion or strength progress by the time of his February exam.

The same was true in March, so Ross wasn't optimistic when he flew to LA for his scheduled exam by Dr. Curtin. Still, he was disappointed to hear Dr. Curtin's candid assessment that it didn't look too good for a successful return to pitching professionally. Dr Curtin told him to keep up his program for three more months at home before returning for a final June visit.

If his recovery wasn't significantly better by then, he suggested that Ross think about a different career. He further suggested that Ross start exploring that possibility while he continued his rehab.

Ross touched base with the Braves' minor league personnel director Reynolds, who informed him that he would continue to get paid through June 30. But if Dr. Curtin's report showed that he might not be able to pitch again...that would be it.

Based upon how Ross was feeling in June, he was not surprised that Dr. Curtin told him that, based upon his still less than full strength and range of motion, he didn't believe that Ross could successfully return to pitching. Ironically, the one guy that Ross would miss the most was Willie, the big black Texan who made sure they got to the various cities and ballparks safe and on time.

This massive-sized, bald-headed man had a sense of humor that kept Ross and the entire Savannah team loose.

Willie would joke, "Hey, you shooting blanks?" his way of kidding the married guys why they didn't have any kids, but the guys loved it when he talked like that. He was a jolly guy until you teased him with a snake.

When the team found out that he feared snakes more than anything else on earth, they bought a rubber snake and threw it at him. They knew enough to get out of the way, because Willie had the power of an NFL running back. Willie also knew immediately when a player had problems, not only the ones on the field, but also the ones off the field. His insights into the other players' issues were uncanny. Some of the pitchers would seek him out for his amazing and rejuvenating massages, those big, powerful hands getting the kinks out.

It had been an exciting two-year's in professional baseball which Ross would remember forever.

Ross knew exactly what he wanted to do. Become an agent to the players. If he couldn't make it as a player, the next best thing was representing them. A front office was not for him, too much ass kissing. He kept close to home attending Triton College in River Grove, IL, a suburb of Chicago.

The best thing about the education is that the Braves were going to pay for it. This was part of the original contract, education after officially retiring from baseball you had 2 years to use the college paid program.

Knowing it takes players about 4 years to make it to the big leagues it would take him every bit of that to get his law degree. Taking basic classes in business education, Ross didn't feel at home in the classroom.

After one-year, Ross decided not to spend 3 more years grinding it out for a law degree. After all, he thought most agents who have players in the big leagues have no law degree. He knew there are no requirements to be an agent, except finding a player who is on the 40-man roster. Pretty simple, find a 40-man guy and then build up from good minor league players.

Ross knew a few from his 2 years in pro ball who have been put on the 40-man roster. Ross purchased the Baseball's Directory. This gave him the complete listing of addresses and schedules for all major and minor league games. He was tempted to call Glenn, but knowing he had Sharpe for his agent, he decided to leave that alone.

It was bye-bye to college and hello to the road and cheap hotels. Ross sort of looked at it as being a scout, you look for talent then try to sign them and represent them, hoping it would pay big dividends later.

6

Spring training in the big leagues is an experience that every baseball player should taste at least once in their career. All the sports equipment companies are there. Glenn got gloves from Rawlings, Wilson, and Mizuno, gathering as many as possible.

He took them back to the minor league complex, giving them out to the guys who really needed them. The Twins liked Glenn since he was a piece of the team they didn't have. Glenn filled in at third, shortstop and second, so his plate was full the entire spring training.

Glenn was surprised to learn how different spring training was for the big leagues. Staying at the upscale players' hotel and making big league money were both very different. Heck, the spring meal money that he received in camp was more than his first year's monthly salary.

Lisa liked spring training camp as well. She got close to some of the players' wives, hitting the pool and taking tennis lessons. Her life felt more fulfilled than in the minors, but she remained in touch with the minor league wives who were part of her bible studies group.

Glenn thought that once you're in the big leagues, you act like a big-leaguer; your life changes quickly, with better restaurants, more dinner parties, and hitting the links. However, the days in camp were long. He would get to the park at 8:00 am, and often left the locker-room at 5:00 pm or later.

Once again, Glenn felt butterflies when Joe Jones, one of his minor league managers and now one of the big league Twins' coaches, came over to his locker and said, "Hey, Skip wants to see you."

Those words can be tough to swallow or music to a player's ears. As he walked toward the manager's office, Glenn reminded himself of his thought at the end of last season, that, no matter what, he was going to have some memorable stories to tell his grandkids.

Sitting behind a big desk was manager Gene Mauch. Glenn didn't get to interact much with him. Glenn's coaching came mostly from other pros on the team. The Twins coaches were a little hesitant to make changes in Glenn's approach to the game; they felt it was better for the veterans on the team to teach him.

Mauch asked him to sit down, then he explained the need for the team to have a solid utility player. He knew that Glenn, like most players, didn't relish being a utility player, a role usually reserved for a veteran guy.

Glenn said, "Whatever the team wants."

Mauch said, "Pack your bags, kid, you're going North with the team!"

"Wow!" Glenn yelled out.

He shook Mauch's hand vigorously. This was not big news to the team, since most of the guys thought that he was going North. They had a surprise waiting for him when he got out of the manager's office – all of his clothes were gone!

He knew this was another prank, finding his shirt, pants, shoes, and socks in the freezer.

Glenn acted like he didn't care, saying, "I'll go buy some nicer ones now that I'm going North with you assholes!"

The guys all laughed, but Lisa was a little surprised, when he came out of the locker room wearing only his practice shorts and shower shoes.

He told Lisa, "Baby, pack your bags for the Twin Cities, we're leaving with the team on a charter flight next week."

They shared a romantic dinner at the Chart House, the two of them in a dream state with a contract for the minimum big-league salary of $35,000.00 over the six-month baseball season. His baseball card in circulation would put more than $9,000.00 per year into their bank account. Glenn ordered another round of appetizers with a smile.

Now that Glenn had his first big league contract, his agent Allen Sharpe became more aggressive in making investments. Breaking camp meant that big dollars would be coming in if all went well. Sharpe met with the Chances during a two-day visit to Minneapolis in the second month of the season.

He outlined a new strategy for investing their money, suggesting lumber, gold mines, and real estate investments. Glenn was more than happy to just play ball and leave the business side of things to him.

Lisa was reluctant to place such trust in Sharpe. She was skeptical of having so much of their money disappear into investments such as land deals, housing and horses. She tried to get Glenn to see Sharpe as a guy to handle contracts only, not to be everything to them – as she put it, a "one stop shop."

Lisa wished now that she had gone to college, maybe to have studied finance or business. How did she know that they would be making so much money this quickly? Lisa asked Glenn at least to inform her of the investments, so she could keep track of them.

She never liked what happened with the first investment, when Sharpe sent Glenn the request to sign the investment documents in late December without having the proper time to question anything. Sharpe also convinced Glenn to sign a power of attorney agreement. This would allow Sharpe to sign documents on Glenn's behalf and to enter into the Chance's investment accounts with freedom to control their finances.

Sharpe convinced Glenn that this was a good thing for them in the long run, saying some investments would have to be made on the spur of the moment. He did think it was cool to invest in a horse farm for breeding, although he knew nothing about horses.

Glenn focused instead on trying to hit the slider, like the one that Ron Guidry of the New York Yankees threw; a pitch that was considered unhittable...unless he made a mistake.

And that is just what happened.

Glenn, hitting eighth in the lineup, got an 86-mph hanging slider from Guidry, hammering it over the left field wall for his first big league home run.

The Yankee left fielder, Rickey Henderson, kept his head up as a fan threw it back to him. Ricky gave it to the umpire, who threw it to the dugout.

Glenn thought about pulling a "Dizzy Trout," but he didn't have the guts to do it. Glenn knew that Detroit Tigers' pitcher Dizzy Trout, after striking out Ted Williams on a full count fastball, had the guts to ask Ted to sign the strikeout ball. The "Splendid Splinter" thought the request so outrageous that he signed the ball, and they became life-long friends. Glenn had his team sign the ball instead.

The rest of the season produced a mixed bag of emotions. Lisa was getting on Glenn's case for being too controlled by Sharpe and too trusting of him. Glenn convinced her that Sharpe was the key to his continuing success at playing baseball, since having such a great agent allowed him to relax. He also told her it was better for them to have someone other than themselves handle their finances, so it was better to just let Sharpe do it.

A minor injury put Glenn on the 15-day disabled list. He broke a finger that got in the way of a fastball on a drag bunt. He was told by the team doctor that it would probably keep him out a couple of weeks.

Glenn didn't think that was too bad, especially after being told by the team trainer that he still gets big league service time while he was on the disabled list, he also still got to travel with the team on road trips.

Glenn usually didn't want to know a team trainer very well, since that would mean that you were spending too much time in the training room. He changed his mind after he started getting treatment from Herm. He learned that Herm was a really cool guy, knowing a number of jazz greats like David Sanborn and Chick Corea.

After coming off the disabled list Glenn played a lot more games at second base, compiling a strong season with a .272 batting average. His defense was still considered good, having made only 3 errors.

Not bad for his rookie season.

Having had a strong first season, Glenn got a radio endorsement contract with a local car dealership.

He told the fans, "Hi fans, I'm Glenn Chance of your Minnesota Twins. I'm usually hitting a baseball all over the park, however, I drive a Chevy everywhere I go!"

The deal was worth $25,000.00 – not bad for a 20-second radio commercial.

Glenn played golf on his days off, so he jumped at the offer from Callaway to have him endorse its new driver. This endorsement brought Glenn another $15,000.00, plus all the free golf equipment he wanted for the next five years.

7

Glenn and Lisa wintered in Florida, with Glenn getting into the best shape of his life. He signed a contract for $75,000.00 for the upcoming season. Substantially higher than last year. Even though it subjected him to accepting the team's offer without much negotiation, Sharpe liked the extra money for investing.

Lisa also brought this subject up with Glenn, asking him if they were giving too much money to Sharpe to invest, especially with no guarantee of any return. As usual, Glenn answered 'no it will be fine." Lisa was cautious, Glenn was more trusting than ever. He tried to cheer her up some by buying the biggest color television available, just in time for them to watch the USA hockey team beat the Russians at the Lake Placid Olympics.

The start of Glenn's second full season was very different than the previous spring. In his mind the big difference was his having that full season of big-league experience under his belt. He told Lisa that he started to feel like part of a family, not just with the Twins, but also the players.

Glenn was making a name for himself in the big leagues. Based upon his performance, he was getting some interest from other agents. One of those agents was MMC, a well-known agency that happened to represent Jerry Koosman, the Twins' star starter. Sharpe got wind of this when someone told him that he saw Glenn having dinner with Koosman and his agents. It took no time for Sharpe to send a nasty letter to Koosman's agents, saying tampering with clients can be very costly.

Sharpe felt pressure from this, so he hung around even more, not only during the summer in Minnesota but also visiting Glenn on road trips. Even though Sharpe had many clients, he never wanted to lose a guy to another agent. Sharpe even hired a former big-league player to coddle his younger clients.

His second full year went by well, even though Glenn never liked his utility player role. Glenn talked to his first base coach and former minor league manager, Joe Jones, about the difficulty of playing third base. Glenn liked playing second base the best.

Johnny told him, "You're doing fine, keep your head up, you can make a lot of money being one of the best utility player's in the league."

Glenn really wanted to be an everyday player. He knew well that a utility player was never respected like an everyday player. For one thing, utility players don't make all-star teams. The Twins promoted a rookie, John Cast, to play third base. Cast developed into the Twins regular third baseman, became their best offensive player, winning Rookie of the Year. So much for becoming the Twins' regular third baseman!

Joe Jones was named Twins manager in late August, replacing Gene Mauch. At the end of the season Twins management asked Glenn to play winter ball in the Dominican Republic. To their surprise, Glenn told them "No," not feeling the need to be a utility player in the D.R. On December 29th Glenn received a thick book from Sharpe, a new prospectus for investment in a car dealership. Lisa immediately reacted, "No way," telling Glenn that "Sharpe already has too much of our money."

In Glenn's mind, reading the prospectus would be a joke and a waste of time, since there was no way that he could understand what it meant. Glenn was advised by Sharpe to sign it right away since the year was ending. He wrote a check for $30,000.00 and Fed-Ex it back to Sharpe's office.

Glenn's third season started poorly. He felt that the Twins organization was upset that he rejected its request to play winter ball in the Dominican Republic. He decided to address the issue with the team to clear the air. He requested a sit-down with Joe Jones, who informed him that it's an honor to be asked to play winter ball. Joe made it clear that the Twins were "all in" for Glenn, that there was no bad blood over the issue, but that next time he should play winter ball.

Glenn knew quite well this season was big, very big. He signed a one-year contract for $85,000.00 while Sharpe began negotiations for a multi-year deal. It could be a two or three-year contract...how sweet would that be?

Things were going well during the season, nothing spectacular, but not too bad either. Sometimes it's best just to ride the wave and not make any splashes. Sharpe told Glenn in mid-July, the Twins were suggesting a contract extension.

Glenn wanted to wait for arbitration while compiling good numbers. Sharpe, on the other hand, wanted Glenn to take a two-year deal if offered, recommending that he grab the money before something bad could happen. Sharpe saw dollar signs, getting his 5% commission on contracts, plus making more on investments.

Glenn and his teammates had to suffer through baseball's first major strike, which interrupted the season for 50 days (June 12-July 31), causing the loss of 713 games.

Glenn and his teammates definitely appreciated the game more after it was taken away from them, but they felt vindicated by staying together, defeating the owners' demand for direct compensation for free agents.

Glenn had fun during one game, with the Twins down 12 runs – they put him in to pitch in the ninth inning. It was a disaster, even with the Boston Red Sox batters actually trying to make outs, making bad swings, or trying to hit the balls right at the fielders.

However, the balls had eyes. Boston scored another six runs. This pitching performance put Glenn in a rare group of players. He knew that he played every position in the infield to close out a year that would likely get him a contract for better money than he'd ever seen.

Sharpe assured Glenn that Minnesota would indeed offer a new contract, a two-year deal for $175,000.00. Glenn happily agreed. He and Lisa were now ready to buy a condo in the Sarasota area. Unfortunately, they would now be making more money than ever and Sharpe was ready to invest more of their money.

Their condo was on Siesta Beach, a soft, white sandy beach of epic beauty. They went on morning runs and in the afternoon, Glenn trained at a local baseball facility. They became regulars at the Chart House restaurant for dinner.

Glenn signed the two-year contract on December 21st, sort of a giant Christmas present from the Twins. Their condo was a great place to spend the winter.

Life was good.

8

Entering his fourth full major league season, Glenn became a hot topic during spring training. Signing a two-year deal assured him some financial freedom. However, this new contract only made Glenn want to do even better, and his intense workouts did not surprise his teammates.

He took early hitting in the cage, often before the other players showed up for practice. Some players have gotten a new multi-year contract, then took it easy, but not Glenn. For example, he worked hard on his bunting, eventually becoming an excellent bunter. Out of his .307 spring training average, 4 of his hits were bunts. He told Lisa that just one or two bunt hits a month could make your average go up considerably, but nobody seemed to do it anymore.

Glenn and his teammates shared extra excitement by starting their season in a new home stadium, the "Metrodome" in downtown Minneapolis.

Glenn's excitement was short-lived in early June. His season changed in a flash when Glenn was driving home after a Friday night game. An illegal drunk driver blew through a red light. and slammed into the driver's side of Glenn's car. After Glenn was finally cut out of the wreckage, he was rushed by ambulance to St. Paul Memorial Hospital.

Lisa received a phone call from the police that Glenn had been involved in an automobile accident – she should go to the hospital immediately. Her emotions ranged from shock to disbelief when she was told that Glenn was being admitted with severe injuries.

He was stabilized in the emergency room and then taken directly to the operating room to repair what they could.

Lisa couldn't decide which was worse, not being able to see him while he was in the operating room or finally being able to see what he looked like when they brought him out of surgery and back to his recovery room.

She could hardly believe it when his orthopedic surgeon arrived, explaining to her that Glenn had sustained a broken left collarbone, multiple cracked ribs, a fractured pelvis, a left leg quad tendon tear, as well as a right elbow injury.

When Glenn was awake enough to realize what had happened to him, he spiraled into a deep depression, seeing all the dreams of his baseball career go right down the drain.

News of Glenn's injuries went out to the media outlets. He and Lisa learned that the driver fled the scene of the accident but was caught blocks away in his stalled car.

Twins players and management made visits to let him know that they were thinking of him. Lisa felt bad when Glenn told her in the hospital, "I'm glad we signed the two-year deal now."

She felt even worse when Sharpe called the next day, boasting, "I bet you're really happy now that I got you that two-year deal!" That call was the only one they got from Sharpe during Glenn's entire hospital stay.

A Minneapolis Star-Tribune reporter interviewed Glenn, since the story was the biggest baseball news the Twin Cities had seen in a long time.

He asked, "Did you see the car before it hit you?"

"No way, man, he blew the red light. I didn't see a thing," he replied.

"What about your career?"

Glenn swallowed hard, saying, "It looks pretty bad from this hospital bed right now, but maybe I can come back stronger than ever."

When Glenn was finally discharged, the team doctors were not too optimistic about his recovery chances. However, they told him that, if he attacked his rehab program with the same determination as his training program, he might stand a chance.

In October, the Twins flew Glenn and Lisa to Florida to start the rehab. Glenn was happy to finally begin this next step of his recovery process while at home. They both felt some sadness leaving the caring doctors, nurses and therapists behind in Minnesota.

To say thank you, Glenn bought a large TV for the employees' cafeteria. Glenn's care, with all of his medical records, was transferred to a well-respected orthopedic surgeon near his home, who was brought up to speed by the Minnesota referring doctors, and would consult with the referring doctors, staying in close touch with the Twins' team surgeon, keeping the team informed along the way.

Glenn called Sharpe's office to let him know of their return to Florida, to brief him on his recovery status, and to set up a meeting for the three of them to go over the status of all of the investments, especially in the face of their uncertain future.

Glenn was actually getting concerned over the amount of time that had passed without any reply from Sharpe.

He was starting to think about all of the conversations he and Lisa had concerning Sharpe over the years and began to feel ashamed about how frequently he had dismissed Lisa's concerns.

Glenn's rehabilitation started at a Sarasota hospital's new rehabilitation center in October. Glenn was transported by wheelchair in a therapy van to and from the rehab center for daily treatment for the first six weeks. The frequency was reduced to three treatments a week for the next six weeks, which took them into 1983.

After these first three months of his rehab therapy had passed, Glenn started to get depressed about the challenge of his recovery. He called Sharpe, but it took Sharpe two weeks to get back to him. Glenn asked Sharpe about the investments, now that it looked like the two-year deal could be the last money that he'll earn in baseball. Sharpe stalled as usual, telling him that he would get the reports for each of his investments sometime soon.

As Glenn's therapy continued, now down to alternating weeks of one visit and then two visits per week, he began to increase his private therapy treatments. He progressed from just walking in his building's pool to actually swimming in it.

With his doctor's approval, he also began light workouts with the strict order not to overdo it. Although Glenn realized there might not be ground balls to field or hanging curveballs to hit for now, he knew that he needed to make sure in his own mind when that would happen.

It was almost the end of summer when Lisa and Glenn finally had a bright spot in their life. Lisa was pregnant. The baby was due in late March next year. Glenn hoped he would be able to provide a nice life for his family.

Glenn's rehab was carefully monitored by the Twins' trainer. They communicated weekly during his therapy. Glenn thought about how we take our health for granted, the simple pleasure of hitting a ball, bending over to scoop up a two-hopper, or even making love to one's wife.

Lisa was very concerned about Glenn's moods, given the medication he was taking. Unlike the kind that Jose Canseco, Barry Bonds, Sammy Sosa, Roger Clemens, and many others in the future were suspected of taking to enhance the body's muscle growth, Glenn's steroids were prescribed directly by the team physician.

Even though the walks were easier on the soft sand of Siesta Key, it was overwhelming to swing a bat, just one swing in the backyard like that in a game at this stage would be a dream.

He worked hard not to burden Lisa, especially since she was showing a growing belly. He dealt with his inner demons, the hate for Hector, the drunk driver, who was working and driving illegally as an undocumented immigrant. He was frustrated with how you can be just a number on the back of a uniform, get hurt, then get dumped by many who you liked.

Glenn was assured of first-class treatment – the players' association gets involved when a player suffers a potentially career-ending injury. But baseball can be hard, it can be politics, it can be business, it can ruin marriages and families. Once the people you believed in turn away, it can cause tremendous grief.

Glenn told the crew at the rehab facility in Sarasota that, with maximum effort, he might have a chance to go to spring training as a player. They all agreed he could, but they were just being polite.

Rehab people know that it was important for the patient to believe and not lose hope. Underneath all of the yes's and "sure you can's," they are all hoping for a miracle.

9

Feeling incomplete without baseball, Glenn was miserable. Heading back to spring training for one last chance to hit the fastball or scoop up a grounder, he tried to be positive, but he also felt some trepidation. The doctors and his rehab team were proud of his hard work and wished him the best.

He pondered "what if'" questions within himself. If I practice too hard, will my body break down? Will pain pills help me heal quicker?

Glenn arrived at the Twins' spring training camp on February 1st, three weeks ahead of the position players' reporting date. He practiced with caution, not trying too hard to make up for lost time. His cage work was strictly for hitting technique. That way, he wouldn't try to hit the ball over the fence, sort of self-controlling his emotions.

Glenn took ground balls at second, fielding 50 grounders a day, just enough to test his broken body while showing his intention of making it back to the big leagues. Glenn knew that baseball is geared to repetition, muscle memory, having as much to do with the mind as with the muscles. He called the brain the most important muscle a player can have.

He told Lisa after the first week how different he was feeling. He remarked that it used to be fun, joking around with the guys. "Now it's just hard, I'm feeling fear, I'm not the same guy," he confessed.

The second week went by with good results. Glenn still took it easy to avoid causing a big problem. The trainers were worried that he might alter his motions, which could worsen his condition. He was not worried about that. He knew that this was the last chance, his comeback opportunity. It was now or never. He pushed himself late into the second week, including taking batting practice on the field.

The training room became his second home, with long hours of treatment. He knew that his future would depend upon being healthy – healthy enough to perform as effectively as before the accident. To Glenn a life without baseball was not worth much. Baseball was all he knew, all he had done since being a kid.

While Glenn was taking on-field batting practice during the third week, a pitcher wanted to see how Glenn would react to a slider, without telling him it was coming. Glenn saw the pitch coming right down the middle of the plate. Feeling stronger, he wanted to test himself by attacking the pitch, wanting to hit it hard, but the ball moved at the last second, darting down and away.

With one swing, altering his repetitive motion, he felt his shoulder pop. The pain was excruciating. He hurried to the training room to pack his shoulder in ice. However, Glenn knew that ice wouldn't be enough.

"It's over, it's all over," he said.

The Twins offered to put him on the 60-day disabled list. Glenn appreciated their offer, but he knew it was time to put baseball out of his mind. It was time to start his life after baseball, and to find out from Sharpe the exact status of all of his investments. He packed his equipment into a duffel bag for the last time.

They returned to Illinois to start their life over, without baseball. It would be better for them to be closer to Lisa's parents especially since Ashley was born in late March. Glenn took a job working at an indoor baseball academy run by a former minor league player. To his surprise, young kids were waiting for him with his baseball card to sign. Glenn also opted for an evening job bartending at a place called *The Last Stop*, a simple place serving pub grub with a good beer selection on tap.

One evening at dinner, Glenn asked Lisa if she still loved him.

"Of course, I love you - what kind of a question is that?" she said.

Glenn explained, "You know, baseball was so much a part of our lives, you made friends, you travel, now look at me, teaching baseball to kids and pouring beer for my old high school teammates."

"We have something now that we didn't have then: our daughter, Ashley. So my life is the best it's been since we fell in love," she assured him.

It was hard to get baseball out of his mind, but it was even harder to get Sharpe out of his mind. There were investments that needed to be disclosed, tax concerns down the road, treatment for an injury to be covered by insurance. It's easy to become unglued when you feel like a failure, when your dreams are stripped away.

Sharpe finally scheduled a meeting with Glenn, if only to get him to stop calling constantly.

Glenn immediately jumped all over Sharpe, demanding an explanation about the lack of information - and especially the *income* - from his many investments. Sharpe reminded Glenn that he needed to be patient because Sharpe had long-term investments designed to pay out money in the long run over his entire lifetime, rather than some short-term schemes that could leave them high and dry later.

For example, Sharpe claimed that the horse farm investments would eventually pay off, since it took time for the farms' sires to become well known and for their foals to prove productive. The real estate buildings took time to rent out and appreciate in value.

Sharpe alleged that he had explained all of this in detail to Glenn at the time. Sharpe also claimed the land deals with the apartment buildings were going to take longer than anticipated, alleging problems due to a contractor's bankruptcy and a steep drop in the real estate market.

He also told them that the lumber forest investments weren't turning any profit currently, since house sales had taken such a downturn.

Sharpe predicted that a car dealership investment in Chicago might pay off after the new year, especially if gas prices dropped, leading new car sales to improve.

After hearing excuse after excuse from Sharpe, Glenn exploded, "I'm tired of hearing nothing but excuses from you. I just want my money back. Why don't you buy me out of all of these investments?"

Sharpe tried to defuse his anger by suggesting, "You're getting the tax write-offs from all of these losses, so you should just ride it out."

Glenn yelled at him, "We need the money now that I'm out of baseball. We need to maintain a lifestyle, especially now with a new baby."

Sharpe told him, "Let me check things out. I'll be in touch."

10

With Glenn's damaged shoulder feeling better, he interviewed for a job with United Parcel Service (UPS). Its big attraction was the benefits package, including health insurance. The manager was delighted to help Glenn out, as he stated during the interview. They discussed what would be best for him as a starting position. They agreed he would start on a package truck, delivering small packages.

One added benefit in Glenn's mind was that it allowed him to work outside and alone, providing him with a certain level of independence. Glenn still wanted to stay connected with baseball, so he shifted teaching baseball lessons to weekends. He believed that with a better-paying job along with health coverage, things were looking up.

On July 30th Glenn met a man on the porch of his house. He gave Glenn a letter identifying him as Joseph Creek of the Internal Revenue Service (IRS).

Glenn read the letter stating that he owed $173,856.00 to be paid by the end of the year. He yelled for Lisa, who hurried into the kitchen, immediately noticing Glenn was very upset. He held up the letter, waving it as if trying to change it from being true.

"Call Sharpe now," he yelled.

Lisa frantically dialed Sharpe's office, but all she got was the message, "Welcome to the best sports representation in the world. Please leave your message."

While he waited three days for Sharpe to return the call, Glenn sank deeper and deeper into depression. When Sharpe returned the call, he informed Glenn that there was little he could do to help, although he offered to speak to Mr. Creek.

"Hell yes," Glenn said. "I want to know why I've got this problem. You said you would be handling our taxes, with our investments paying off when I stopped playing."

Glenn started to miss a few of his UPS pickups, as his mind was in the clouds with the tax problem. Lisa became increasingly worried about Glenn, noticing him becoming more temperamental.

He told himself, "The only things I've got are Lisa and Ashley."

He worried how he would support the two of them. Could he still be a good husband and father? Lisa told him, "You're making too much of this. We'll be fine. We have each other. Don't forget that."

He thought first of Allen Sharpe, then of Hector, the illegal, uninsured drunk driver, with hatred.

"What am I going to do? I wanted Lisa to have the life of a big leaguer. Nice cars, a place on the beach, expensive dinners, and Ashley having the best of the best."

Sharpe got back to Glenn after talking to Creek, telling Glenn that there was nothing Creek would do to help him out. Glenn was overwhelmed, hearing that his bank account would be levied beginning next month.

The IRS Form CP297 came, informing Glenn he had 30 days to respond. Sharpe told him this was not his problem, suggesting that he get a good tax lawyer. Glenn called up his tax accountant to vent about his tax crisis, only to be informed by a secretary that the accountant was out of town for the next 9 days.

Glenn was distraught. He began calling Sharpe daily without response. Lisa became very concerned, feeling that Glenn was becoming unglued. They worried about the money, the IRS being a group of thugs with governmental power. He conceded it probably wasn't the IRS' fault. He just wanted answers; now was the time for Sharpe to tell him.

Glenn called the Major League Baseball Players Association for help, but he only got the runaround. They told him they couldn't get involved between a player and his agent.

Glenn responded by asking them, "Who do you take care of, the players or the agents?"

Glenn developed a strong sense of distrust. The Association, to which he had paid monthly dues for years, was supposed to be this strong union working on behalf of the players, but it seemed they were more interested in protecting the agents. He thought, "Why didn't the union protect the players from bad agents that many players reported?" He heard about the chief of the union recommending players to agents who turned out to be fraudulent with their fiduciary responsibilities. There were also financial institutions getting a heads up to invest free agents' big bonus signings.

Sharpe finally got back to Glenn, only to tell him one final time that the tax issue was not his problem. He suggested that the IRS was a tough team to get out, so why not just try to work with them?

An IRS meeting was set up with Glenn and his accountant. They walked out with a good feeling, since the IRS agent had been polite and somewhat receptive to Glenn's request to open up years of alleged tax debt. However, the next visit resulted in little relief. The tax amount owed was still staggering, especially with high interest accruing.

He felt emotionally and financially bankrupt, as well as increasingly isolated.

11

In the meantime, Ross spent a large amount of time in December trying to finalize locations for his Spring Training 1982 Agent Days. The Pittsburgh Pirates were the first team to agree to host an Agent Day at their Bradenton, Florida spring training site. Ross planned to visit the Cubs in Arizona and then travel back to Florida.

Ross agreed with the Pirates to host a table during their two-hour Agent Day in March. Once he got the Pirates to agree, other teams considered the idea. He shared the idea with General Manager Dallas Green of the Chicago Cubs and Manager Jim Frey, who suggested he talk with their minor league director.

The director had a simple response: "Wait till next year." But the Chicago White Sox and the New York Mets came on board. About a month prior to spring training, Ross took time out to watch his Chicago Bears pulverize the New England Patriots 46-10 in Super Bowl XX.

Ross was able to group his three Florida Agent Days into a March week. Ross started with the White Sox in Sarasota. He met with the Sox General Manager Roland Hemond, who had been the Sox GM since 1970. Ross also enjoyed his conversation with Manager Tony LaRussa after the Sox workout, while the tables and chairs were being set up. He talked with LaRussa about being a lawyer. Tony went to

Florida State University College of Law, being admitted to the Florida bar in 1980.

Ross had been looking forward to the Pirates' "Agent Day," since it had been the first team to agree to host an Agent Day session. He probably would have been surprised to learn that the players and coaches had been talking about Agent Day during the hours before the agents set up their tables and met with the players.

In the bullpen two coaches asked each other if they were going.

Coach Whitey: "Sure am, I want to see these so-called agents who are after the kids' money. The agents are making some serious cash on these guys, they hardly do anything for them anyway. They pile up some statistics on a computer and make a phone call to the GM to get the contract done. The biggest part of their job is to take the owners to arbitration and hope for a win, getting the 5% they charge the player. They just use the players to live the life they want, feeling important hanging around the athletes. Some of the scum agents even charge 50% of the Latin kids' money."

Coach Razor said, "Okay, Whitey, how do you really feel?"

"Well, Razor, I feel even worse about how the agents are ruining the game. I think they try to get the players to go against the organizations that give the kids a chance to make it in baseball. They truly don't care a damn about the kids or the team. As soon as the player gets hurt or stops making money, they turn their backs on the player faster than Ricky Henderson stealing a base or a Nolan Ryan fastball."

"Speaking of fastballs, that Lefty has a great arm, not bad for a 33rd rounder."

"Does he have an agent?"

"Yeah, he sure does; he'll pitch in the big leagues someday. His agent was here the other day with a white poodle on a leash. It was the first time the kid had met him in person. When I teased Lefty about the poodle, he said, 'My agent's lucky I like dogs.'"

It was about 2:00 PM, so now it was time to meet the agents.

Lefty said, "Hey, Snake, what about Agent Day, you going?"

Snake said, "Hell no, me and the Snake," as he held and twirled his junk around in a circle, "are heading to the beach. It's spring break. You gotta get it while it's hot."

The farm director was talking to the field coordinator, both were interested in meeting the group of agent companies.

Butch said, "Hey, Stick, maybe we should get an agent. You know, we should be represented too."

Stick said, "Hell, our job is only as good as the talent we get, just hired to get fired. I know what you are saying, Butch, but in the minor leagues it is not as much about the talent as it is about babysitting the bonus babies. Sometimes I feel our hands are tied – when we have to reprimand a player, they want us to be so careful not to hurt their egos. I had to talk to one player and convince him not to go home. Hell, he got a $750,000.00 signing bonus, and he asked me if it's guaranteed. I asked him what the problem was, and he said he missed the simple life with his girlfriend."

"It sure is hard to judge the heart of a player."

"Yeah, then I said, 'Hey, when you get to Double AA ball, you will change your mind. The girls in Tennessee will make you forget her, as long as they don't make you forget how to hit a slider.'"

"Being the farm director, I have to talk to all those agents. How I hate to talk to them - they are dollar chasers. They are truly thieves. No less than an ambulance chaser, they only see dollar signs in the kids. Anyone can call themselves an agent; there are no restrictions on who can represent a player. In the big leagues, they might soon have a requirement, but they should do something about the minor league side of the game. So many players get their agents in minor leagues and feel loyal to them. If they do make it, their agents often take advantage of them."

Stick, grabbing his clipboard, followed Butch out to the field.

Stick said, "You can bet the Players Association knows of many bad agents who have stolen from the players. Someone told me the PA has an internal system of keeping the problems away from the media. If word got out about how corrupt agents are, fans would see that the agents are as greedy as Wall Street. There was some talk that a head Players Association guy even recommended financial firms to new bonus babies, then got a kickback. That's some heavy shit, if it's true."

The outfield had seven folding tables with hungry agent companies behind them. Players could go up to any table to see what they were all about. Lefty made his way toward his agent; he was able to find him easily due to the barking poodle.

Lefty said, "Hello, Mr. Castle, what's up?" Castle said, "Lefty, you looked great today in the pen."

"Yeah, but don't forget it's only the bullpen, not a real game."

"Sorry I never made it to Lynchburg to see you last season, but I was trying my best to follow you in the Sporting News."

"Hey, at least you got me my shoes and the glove contract, but you know that's not what I really want from my agent anyway."

"Don't worry about a thing, you just get the ball over the plate, let me handle all the business matters, that's my game."

There must have been about thirty players walking from table to table.

Table 1 - A law firm that boasted, "We negotiate with anyone from criminals to ball players." The humor seemed to work as they signed up two players right away. This law firm talked about unionizing the minor leagues. "Hey, if you play for 10 years in the minors and never get a chance in the bigs, you should get some compensation for the entertainment you provided for all those hard years." The players agreed.

Table 2 - "Latins for Latinos." They made no bones about it. There were six guys, and their families were all around. Naturally, this group seemed very popular with the Latino players, who were notorious for having four or five agents, some having doctored birth certificates. American players joked that a Latin player was 18 going on 25.

Table 3 – A husband-and-wife team had some Bibles out in the open, a picture of Jesus in a baseball uniform, and a slogan, "Saving players, not games – give your heart to Jesus." They did get two players to stop and bow their heads as they prayed.

Table 4 - King, Oakley and Jackson. "We always got your back. We stand in front of the rest because we are the best. We give "soul" support." It was pretty obvious who their target audience was. Many of the African American players were talking to them. Some players were happy to see some "brothers in the business." One player said, "It's about time some of us got into the agent game." They handed out business cards, inviting players to visit them at the Holiday Inn for dinner.

Table 5 - Ross Borgia set up with a simple display of his brochures, as well as a picture of him in his playing uniform when he was a minor leaguer with the Atlanta Braves. He talked to players, letting them know he was once a player, but when he didn't make it due to injury, he went to school to get his college and law degrees. You can trust me to "do the right thing," he had printed on the business card. His slogan was "Right vs. wrong, right wins." He also let the players know that it was his idea to make Agent Day happen.

Table 6 - Two attorneys and a staff of Hooter girls got most of the attention. They actually owned a couple of franchises and now wanted to be glorified babysitters. This table had the players and the coaching staff hanging out at it. They were handing out free wing coupons, tee shirts, hats, and autographs from the girls. One Hooter girl gave her t-shirt to a player in exchange for his practice jersey. The player sniffed deeply into the t-shirt, then smiled at the other guys.

One player asked, "Hey, where do I sign up?" A girl whipped out a contract, which he signed and got a free Hooters calendar. She pointed to her picture in the lower right-hand corner, jotting her phone number down next to her cleavage.

Another player said out loud, "What do you do for a birthday boy - I ain't got no agent?" The lawyers said, "We'll take you and your teammates to dinner at Hooters and then to the Cheetah Lounge."

The players high-fived each other, as if they'd won a playoff game. Obviously, they liked the idea. They established a meeting time of 7:00 PM. The birthday boy and his friends were going out for a night on the town. As promised, the night finished at the Cheetah Lounge. The birthday boy got a lap dance by all of the working girls, while one player called his wife, telling her that he was horny and missed her.

Table 7 - Excellence in Sports, Inc. The company boasted about having everything under one roof. "One stop shopping." Players could have their accounting done, investments, concert tickets, and travel all arranged for them with a phone call. The table was piled high with Nike shoes, Reebok batting gloves, Rawlings gear, and other tools of the trade. Many players liked this setup, with a few signing up. At the conclusion of the Pirates Agent Day session, Ross headed back to the Tampa airport for his return flight to Bloomington.

12

All was not well with Lisa on Sunday night. She was wondering if her husband was really on a fishing trip with his two best buddies. She had just received a phone call from one of those buddies to see if Glenn was home.

Lisa was shocked, "Mark, I thought you guys were on a fishing trip." She was beside herself. She made frantic phone calls to his other friends. However, one friend's wife said, "No, John was asked by his company to go to Houston for business."

Lisa said, "So you are sure he isn't on a fishing trip with Glenn?" She assured Lisa that her husband was in Houston.

Lisa said, "Something is wrong, and I'm very worried. He's never done anything like this before. He's always been truthful with me."

Lisa started to think of many what-ifs. All attempts to reach him were unsuccessful. Could it be another woman? Did he leave us? What if he had a bad accident and is lying by the side of a road? Many mental images ran through her mind - the changes in Glenn's life after baseball, his troubles with past investments, his anger against his agent.

Glenn was well aware of what was on his mind as he checked into the Motel 6 next to *Sports Authority* on the service road near his modest home. He parked his car in back to keep it from being seen. Check-in was done quickly.

He requested one thing – the key to room 17, his old baseball number. He wanted it that way. He unlocked the door with one of those new credit card versions of a room key. Motel 6 has certainly upgraded their amenities, he laughed.

He still had a sense of humor even under the bleak upcoming endgame of his emotions. He had with him a bottle of tequila, a notepad and a gun. He felt lonely and ashamed. Tonight, he would drink and drown his sorrows in what could be his last night alive. He felt for his family, but his despair was so overwhelming that nothing could fill the void he felt.

Glenn's world changed after several years of investing in complicated tax shelters, finally drawing the attention of the IRS. He was shocked when the IRS agent met him on his porch. He got no satisfaction from Sharpe, who just blew him off. Glenn had the IRS papers sitting next to him on the bed. His anger, frustration, regret, and guilt had finally devastated him.

He said to himself, "I never should have blindly trusted my agent. I should have put all my money in the bank. I should have listened to Lisa."

He poured a glass of tequila and started writing. His letter was a confession of the guilt he felt from his financial failure, his anguish toward the IRS bill for the enormous amount of $173,856.00, and his complete failure for trusting his agents with all of his baseball money.

Glenn felt that Sharpe was the real reason for this sad situation. He had tried to reach him, but Sharpe had returned very few calls in the last six months. Glenn made one last call to Allen's office, only getting the answering machine. Realizing it was Sunday night, Glenn left a message that he'd better call him at 11:00 AM on Monday.

Glenn wrote in the suicide letter stories about the investments and some of the things Allen had done to him. He wrote how he was led like a horse with blinders, the type used by guides through very narrow trails, where the horses would never tread unless they were manipulated. He wrote of how he was concerned, but Sharpe always said, "Just trust us, hold tight—when you're done playing ball, you will love us even more." These agents had more tricks up their sleeves than Harry Houdini.

He wrote of his deep love for Lisa and Ashley. He mentioned the insurance policy that he hoped would help with the IRS amount owed. He felt overwhelmed. Pouring another glass of tequila to help him fight the demons, he lit up a cigarette and turned the TV on as he drank himself to sleep.

Glenn woke up as the maid opened the door.

"Didn't you see the damn 'Do Not Disturb' sign?"

Glenn felt bad. She quickly shut the door without comment. At 11:00 AM, Glenn dialed Sharpe's number.

"Hello, Allen Sharpe's office, Michelle speaking."

Glenn yelled, "Put me through to Allen."

"May I ask who's calling?"

"It's Glenn Chance," as he poured a glass of Tequila.

"I'm putting you through now."

Allen said, "Hey, Glenn, what's the problem? I generally don't get old clients telling me I'd better call them, or else."

"First, why haven't you returned most of my phone calls these last six months?"

"The last few months have been hell, and the IRS shit is too thick to cut through. I did call you to let you know that."

"What about all of my other calls? Why do I have to hunt you down?"

"Look, Glenn, when I represented you, I did the best I could, and the investments you made with us gave you tax breaks and some returns. The IRS problems are just as bad for us as they are for you. I can't babysit you anymore. Heck, I'm busy with new clients. I can't help that a player's career is short-lived. My career as an agent continues, and frankly, I've got more clients than ever."

"Yeah, I helped you get a few of them."

"Oh, Glenn, don't even go there."

"Go there? I'm there. I'm so there that some of that shit you pulled on us was more about your empire than us as people. You took advantage of us – you knew you could, and you did."

"Those are some pretty strong allegations. So be it, it's over with."

"Hey, scum bag, we're in some real trouble with the IRS. Since you got us into this mess, we want you to get us out of it."

"That will be impossible for me to do. I simply cannot help you. You're no longer a client. Look, you don't pay us a fee anymore, now you want me to help you? You've done your own taxes since you left our firm, so it's best if you just keep everything the way you want it, with me and my company out of your life."

"Well, we're not out of *your* life. I'm going to make sure everyone sees you for who you really are, a scumbag in a suit. When this is over, everyone will know the truth."

Allen switched to the speakerphone and stood up, pacing his office.

"What do you mean, when this is over?"

"I only see one way out of this, Allen, and the only thing that will save my family is if I'm not here to add to their struggle. Maybe they will benefit if I'm gone."

"Don't do anything stupid."

"No, I already did that when I trusted you with all those investments."

Glenn fondled the gun, putting one bullet in the chamber, holding it to his temple.

"I wrote a letter that I'm leaving here in the room at Motel 6, and when they find it, I'm sure you will be getting many phone calls."

"What letter? You're getting to be a real pain in the ass. You can't threaten me. I'm done talking to you about your problems. Don't call me anymore."

Holding a picture of the family, Glen pulled the trigger. As the sound penetrated Allen's office, he knew what had happened. He yelled back at Glenn, but Glenn's problems were over.

As the gunshot still echoed, Allen hung up. He called Motel 6, asking where they were located.

He hurried to the hotel.

13

The trip from Peoria was about a two-hour drive. On his arrival at the motel, Sharpe was surprised that there was no police presence there, but it was only 5 pm and no one at the motel knew what had happened. Deciding to play it safe, he parked his car down the block, then walked back to its office. He asked the desk clerk, Amy, for Glenn Chance's room number, and she gave him the spiel that it was against Motel 6 policy to give out personal information. When Allen quickly whipped out a crisp 50-dollar bill, Amy handed him a key to room 17.

Allen opened the door, and saw Glenn's legs on the bed. As he entered further, he saw the motionless body with blood from a self-inflicted head wound. Allen made quick work gathering the papers, the letter, and the envelope next to the tequila bottle. He made no effort to see if Glenn was breathing or to check for signs of a pulse, but simply opened the letter.

After reading, he thought to himself how this could have caused a lot of serious problems. He lit a match, burned the pages of the letter in the bathroom sink, flushing the ashes down the toilet. Allen believed that he had left nothing to be found by the police that would incriminate him. He shut the door while leaving the 'Do Not Disturb' sign on the outside of the door. He walked directly back to his car, driving straight to Peoria.

After time passed, the desk clerk's curiosity got the best of her, so she made her way to the room. She knocked three times, saw the sign, and finally opened the door. She screamed seeing Glenn lying there covered in blood, then quickly called 911.

She worried afterward that she might have contaminated potential evidence. After the police arrived, she gave them all the information, including Glenn's registration information and a description of the man who visited his room.

The police began their fingerprint investigation, and, after the body was removed, they sealed off the room as a crime scene. Amy called the police the next day, telling them she had noticed a burnt smell in the room.

A team of detectives drove to Lisa's home, giving her the terrible news of Glenn's suicide. She collapsed into one of the detective's arms.

Filled with shock and grief, she explained that he had become increasingly distraught due to long-term problems with his agent and the large IRS tax debt he had caused them.

She gave them Sharpe's Peoria address, but, since it was two hours away, it didn't seem to be of immediate interest to them.

The police called Sharpe the next day, but he only mentioned Glenn's Sunday night voicemail message, and his Monday morning call that was very heated with him and hanging up on Glenn.

14

Mattoon, Illinois is in the central part of the state; its love for baseball was well known. Its high school baseball teams often were in the state finals. Very good players from Mattoon have gone on to pro ball. The population is under 28,000, and most of them are talking about the LHP phenom who could be the number one player in the June amateur draft this year. Some say this could put Mattoon back on the baseball map.

Since today is the day for the final qualifying game, the teams arrive early, as do the scouts and agents. Closer to game time, the parents, friends, farmers in overalls, most of whom don't necessarily go to games, are showing up. This is a big deal to the town; everyone was ready to cheer on their local hero. Folding lounge chairs are lined up along the baseline fences. However most scouts stand in back of the home plate area.

The scouts stay in small packs, but the ones who have been around - salty old timers - make their rounds and the bullshit starts flying. They really do love to get together, as the scouts are the hardest-working guys in the game. They are the ones who know the talent and have the greatest influence on a team's success.

The old-timers are the most respected, as everyone likes to hear their stories. Along with the herd of scouts are a few agents; you can't go anywhere without agents being there. There are fewer agents than most would think at this game, but, when you have a player of Trevor Redman's caliber, most agents don't even attempt to go after him.

Some of the big agents send bird dogs as gofers, who try to find out everything about a kid and to meet the family members. Gofers are like the cat that wants to impress the owner with his skills, like bringing home a dead mouse. They don't know jack about baseball, so they often talk with scouts to get a "read" on a player.

The scouts positioned themselves by the bullpen, waiting for Trevor to start his warm-up pitches. They watch everything: his pregame routine, how he stretches, they dissect every move he makes. One scout said, "He's free and easy, nice finish at the end, good life with some tail, his ceiling is high." A rookie scout said, "He's sneaky fast." Back Roads, a veteran scout, said, "Shit, nothing sneaky about 92 with life."

The cross-checkers are the ones who make the big decision on how much the team will spend on the draft choice, so they're watching with intense scrutiny. One scout said, "I heard that some teams will pay up to 2 million for his name on a contract."

The coach asked some of the scouts to move over a little, because there's little room for his teammates to look at some of the pitches in the batter's box. Some scouts were evaluating Trevor's body. One scout said, "What kind of heart does he have?"

Another said, "That is the hardest thing to project - you really can't evaluate his heart until he goes through the hard stuff of trying to make it to the big leagues."

The veteran scout said, "He'd be better off not having a heart."

They questioned his mental makeup; all lefties are treated that way.

"He's soft," a rookie scout said.

Trevor finished his last warm-up fastball, adding a little extra to it, then walked past the scouts dreaming of signing him.

At the bullpen area, Ross introduced himself to another agent, "Hi, I'm Ross Borgia. Who are you here to see?"

Arnie said, "Come on, I'm here to see the same kid we're all here to see."

"Well, good to meet you, what's your name?"

"Arnie Doubleday."

"Any relation to Abner? Just kidding."

Arnie didn't crack a smile; instead he just walked away with a don't follow me attitude.

Ross saw a scout he remembered from when he was pitching in Clarksville.

Ross said, "Hi, Back Roads, you remember me?"

Back Roads smiled. "Heck yeah, you were on my list one time as a kid to follow, but I saw that the Braves drafted you."

"It's good to see you are still scouting."

"Yeah, I'm still doing the maggot work. What about you, Ross?"

"After I hurt my arm I went to college, then I got my degree in sports law. I'm on the other side of the fence from you. I'm starting an agent business, hope you don't mind that."

"Hell no, the game needs good guys like you. Good luck, I can see you have competition out here with this other agent."

Back Roads pointed to Arnie.

"He works for Allen Sharpe, one of the big companies, but he don't know a thing about the game. He's an insurance salesman for his real job."

"Hell, a little competition never hurts, bring 'em all on."

"Did you hear about Glenn Chance?"

"What do you mean?"

"He blew his brains out in a hotel room yesterday."

Back Roads handed Ross the sports section of the newspaper.

"Oh my God," Ross sputtered as he read the article in disbelief.

He immediately walked towards the parking lot.

The news of Glenn's death left him in such a state of hurt that the game had no interest for him anymore.

Back on the field, Trevor started to mow down the opposing batters the same way a superior animal kills its weaker prey.

Arnie saw this with dollar signs. He stared at the pitcher's mound but then turned and stalked the crowd. He needed to find Trevor's parents.

"Hey, Nick," Arnie asked the old-time scout, who was chewing on the end of an unlit cigar proudly wearing a California Angels hat, "can you point out Trevor's family for me?"

Nick replied, "Well, he ain't got no dad, but over there with that blanket over her shoulders is his mom."

Arnie saw that she was easy to find, the only Black mother sitting in the stands.

He asked Nick, "What happened to the father?"

Nick said, "He got kicked in the head by his own horse and died three years ago in a barn."

The game was going very smoothly for Trevor; however, Arnie was more interested in meeting his mom. He waited for the right time to strike, like a boxer does when the opponent lets his guard down.

Arnie was feeling comfortable since hearing the father was deceased. He knew in a selfish way that it was to his advantage that Mrs. Redman was a widow.

Arnie made his introduction. It was not unusual for Mrs. Redman to have agents coming up to her, so she was polite and in a good mood, mostly due to Trevor's wonderful pitching performance.

Arnie said, "Hi, Mrs. Redman, my name is Arnie Doubleday."

Mary said, "Any relation to Abner?"

Arnie laughed as if he'd never heard the joke before and handed her his business card. He praised Trevor then, going right in for the kill.

"Mrs. Redman, let me be frank. Trevor is going to make a lot of money in the June draft. If you give us a call, we will get him top-dollar. By the way, my home number is on the back of the card. We can make it so Trevor gets a record-breaking signing bonus. Let's set up a lunch date with your husband so we can talk about what we do as a sports agency."

"Mr. Doubleday, my husband died three years ago when he was working in the barn."

"What happened? Did a horse kick him in the head or something?"

"Yes. That is exactly what happened. He was cleaning out the stall. I found him a few hours later with the horse pulling at his shirt."

"Mrs. Redman..."

"Oh, just call me Mary."

"Mary, I'm so sorry about that, but please let me talk to you about how much money Trevor is going to demand. His name on a contract will be worth millions. You know your husband is up there watching over everything anyway."

They returned to watching the game. By now, it was within two outs of being over - one of Trevor's most dominating displays of his gifted left arm.

"Mary, I'll let you go, but please call me for lunch. Mr. Sharpe and I would love to take you for lunch. We can give you good representation."

Mary nodded her head as Arnie walked over to where the scouts were for the last out of the game, another strikeout for Trevor.

Arnie asked a scout from Minnesota, "Do you think the kid is that good?"

The scout said, "Yeah, he's that good, so good it takes us out of the bidding. There is no way we can compete with the big clubs. Minnesota ain't got that kind of glue."

The umpire raised his right arm, showing off his style with a called strike three on a curveball that left the hitter shaking his head. All the hitter could do was stand in the batter's box and check his underwear. He watched as Trevor's teammates surrounded him as they walked off the field.

Arnie made his way toward the right field corner, since the teams had to exit from there. Arnie timed this so that he met Trevor at the gate.

Arnie said, "Hey, lefty, nice game, you just made yourself a millionaire. I met your mother and she is a wonderful lady. I hope she gives me a call. Did you have your best stuff today?"

Trevor shook his head no. Arnie pointed to his black Corvette with a soft white top.

"This is what you could be driving if you let us represent you."

Trevor's teammates asked, "How many agents does that make?"

Trevor explained, "Oh, I let my mom take care of all that."

Trevor watched Arnie drive off, his eyes glued to the speeding sports car.

15

Ross was distraught at the news of Glenn's death, finding it hard to believe. He wondered why this happened. Ross knew Glenn. Their paths hadn't crossed recently, but they had been high school teammates and friends.

With news of the tragic death swirling in Ross's mind, he decided to go see Lisa Chance. Ross drove his white Ford to her house on Pleasant Street in Clarksville. Five rings brought Lisa to the door.

Ross immediately expressed his condolences. He watched as Ashley pulled on her mom's leg, asking, "Is it Daddy?"

Lisa picked up Ashley.

Ross listened as Lisa acknowledged her grief. He offered to come back another day, but she asked him to stay.

"Well, Lisa, as soon as I heard the news about Glenn, I drove right over to see what I could do to help."

He explained that he heard the scouts talking about the tragic news at the game. He told her that he was now representing players and maybe he could help if she needed anyone.

Ross said that he realized how people can become lost when life throws a nasty curveball at them. Lisa nodded her head.

Lisa let her guard down when Ross pulled out his business card that read: "Ross Borgia: Law and baseball go together." Ross offered his services, asking whether Glenn had continued to use Allen Sharpe as his agent.

Lisa invited him to stay, making two cups of instant coffee. Ross felt this was his chance to make a name for himself, since he sensed something shady in Glenn's suicide.

Ross had heard about many cases of agents misrepresenting players, with laws being broken like bats shattered by a Nolan Ryan fastball. Ross explained that there was much that could go undetected by a spouse, as Ashley clamored for Lisa's attention. Lisa talked about how they went through the hard times and the good times, but she never thought Glenn was so disturbed.

"He told me everything. We had no secrets; we just wanted to have a small family and be happy. We were even thinking of growing chickens and herbs and opening up our own small farmers' market. He's all I had. I have no immediate family. My mom and dad died recently while traveling overseas, and I was the only child. Glenn was my everything."

Ross started off by asking Lisa what she thought happened that would have caused Glenn to take his life.

"All was going well. Sure, Glenn missed the game and the guys, but seemed otherwise okay. The doctors said that the traffic accident came close to killing him, but the final shoulder injury ended his comeback hope. He was doing well at his UPS job, driving a truck, and he was starting to make better money."

"Didn't Glenn make about half a million dollars playing ball?"

"We did good, but Sharpe had us investing in whatever he said, like land deals, horse farms, gold mines, oil wells, limited land partnerships, all kinds of stuff. All I know is there were never any returns on our investments.

"No, Lisa, I'm sure some of them made money. But the big question that I hope to find out is: Who ultimately *got* the money?"

Lisa became calmer, and they went over a sample agreement that Ross had in his briefcase.

He told her he would have an agreement typed up and mailed to her and she should feel free to have an attorney review the agreement before she signed it.

If he was able to discover fraudulent activity and financial abuse by Sharpe's agency and recovered money, then his fee would be based upon a percentage of the amount recovered.

Lisa followed Ross out to his car with Ashley in her arms.

He got into his Ford, rolling down the window to say, "Hang in there, we'll get to the bottom of this."

Lisa was glad to have Ross represent her and realized that she had nothing to lose.

While Ross pulled away, he continued to watch Lisa, who faded away in the rear-view mirror, as did the smile on his face. It turned into a squint, as if he knew he was going to be in a fight; the fight of a lifetime.

Back at his lake house, Ross started sorting through Glenn's investment books, prospectuses, and tax returns. It took some time to organize the sea of paperwork.

He saw that the relationship the Chances had with the Sharpe sports agency stank of avarice and neglect...a shell game of greed. He hired an attorney friend to help sort it all out.

Ross decided to make a surprise appearance at Sharpe's office. He felt that this was the smart tactic; the element of surprise could stir up emotions or lead to something interesting. He drove to Peoria and parked in the back of the building.

When he entered the office, a beautiful girl named Michelle asked, "Can I help you?"

"Of course you can, I'm here to see Allen Sharpe."

"Did you make an appointment?" asked Michelle.

"No, but I'm willing to wait until tomorrow if it takes that long to see him," said Ross.

Ross took a seat next to a large TV set, listening to ESPN.

Michelle got up from her desk and headed into the office, which had a large sports jersey on the door with "SHARPE" stenciled on the back.

When she came back out she asked, "What's the purpose of the meeting?"

"Just tell him I'm representing Lisa Chance."

As Michelle came back the second time, she said, "Allen will see you in a few minutes."

Ross tried to make small talk with Michelle during the wait, and at times she responded with a few words herself. However, she was busy with the phone ringing and paperwork.

She answered the phone and said, "He's ready."

Michelle showed Ross to the office, as Sharpe was standing at the door. Michelle noticed neither one wished to shake hands as she shut the door.

The office was like a museum with jerseys, a Wheaties box with Sharpe's face on it, bobble head dolls, and a contract for ten million dollars he had negotiated. Ross chuckled at Sharpe's narcissism.

"Okay, so you are handling the affairs of Glenn's death and representing Lisa," said Allen.

"That's right and I'm sure you are aware of how he died. I've been hired by Lisa to look into the investments and other business dealings you had them involved in. Or should I say you got them to buy into. I was hoping we could go over a few investments."

"Look, I'm not in a position to talk to you now or even later about this former client. Glenn went on his own a couple of years ago, deciding to do his own taxes. We all moved on from each other. His investments became his own problems," said Allen.

"Oh, yeah, Lisa will never see what is coming down the road with those tax shelters. There is a huge tax problem; I believe that's why Glenn killed himself."

"Hey, I have no idea what happened that night, and I'm getting pretty pissed off at you insulting my integrity. Let me tell you, Ross, that I have no time left for this conversation. If you want to know more do your investigation," said Allen.

Sharpe walked to the door and asked Michelle to show Ross out.

"No worries, Allen, I will be calling you again soon, because I have many questions regarding the Chances."

On his way out, Ross mentioned to Michelle he would call her when he got back from Florida. He said he hoped that she had no bad feelings about what happened today.

16

Back in Mattoon, Allen Sharpe, Arnie Doubleday, and Mrs. Redman were having lunch. The lunch was arranged by Allen, who told Michelle to call him at the restaurant every 15 minutes during lunch. Mrs. Redman was a very nice lady who realized that it was time to start talking to agents about her son. The high school coach was easily persuaded by Doubleday to recommend Sharpe to be their agent, with a promise of two World Series tickets.

During lunch Allen took the lead, putting on a show. This was his chance to make the big pitch. He schmoozed her with empathy over her husband's death. He mentioned how hard it must be to live in a small town without being able to go out and live a little. She acknowledged the lack of interesting things to do there then Allen excused himself to take a phone call.

He came back with a story of a client in need of travel arrangements for his family. Michelle made the calls as instructed, but she knew something was shady. Allen had his briefcase with him. The contracts had been prepared and Mrs. Redman signed. During dessert they toasted their new partnership. Allen offered to show her his office in Peoria, that is, if she would like to get away. "Come up to Peoria and let me show you around." They agreed on a time for next week.

After getting back from Florida, Ross dug deeper into the investments. He called Michelle at the office. She was not very receptive, until he used Lisa and Ashley as bait to have a drink with him at Bennigan's. She agreed to see him on Friday after work.

Ross sent the investment documents to an accounting firm he hired to investigate. He asked them to look for any misrepresentations or areas of fiduciary misconduct that might have occurred. He also asked them to look at the investments to see who was really making money on them. The accounting firm, Mark Fingers and Company, looked for names of the investors and its general partners. There was a lot to cover, so they were going to need time and perhaps a trip to Sharpe's other office in Beverly Hills California.

They met at Bennigan's restaurant with the conversation going better than either one expected. Michelle liked Ross's approach and his looks weren't bad either, she thought. She was impressed that he had played minor league ball. When he knew he wasn't going to make it, he went and got an education. He liked her intelligence, her beauty, her knowledge of baseball. She said, "I knew I had to learn something about sports, especially baseball, if you're going to work for a big agent like Sharpe." She also mentioned that working for him was a personal challenge.

"He's always trying to hook me up with his clients, even if the guy is married, and he's always making comments about my body," said Michelle.

"How about a sexual harassment lawsuit?" asked Ross.

"I know this might sound funny, but I don't believe in all that crap. If a man compliments you, just accept it. As long as he doesn't touch me, I can tolerate a comment or two. Sports brings on a different mentality working with athletes."

Ross liked this beautiful woman even more. He started talking about his trip to Florida for Agent Day. Then he set the hook for Michelle to help him get some important information about Sharpe.

"Michelle, you know that I'm representing Lisa Chance, and this situation is most difficult because she has no knowledge of the investments. I've already found some red flags in the paperwork that look very suspect, but I need some of the original prospectus documents saying which people are partners and who manages the money. There are names of companies, but I need to know who manages them. I think it is Sharpe who owns all of it. Even if it's all legitimate, there is still an ethical responsibility that Sharpe had to the Chances. It's called 'fiduciary responsibility.'"

"Exactly what is it that you want me to do? I don't want to get in trouble."

"I would like to see copies of the original prospectuses that he sent to the Chances for their investments. I want to go where he goes, see how he works, be on his back, be on him like white on dice," said Ross.

"All of Allen's travel plans go through a travel agency, but I have all the information about his destinations. I know he's planning a trip to the Dominican Republic next week."

"Yes, Michelle, that's what I want. Heck, I will be on that flight with him, stay where he stays, and see the players he is there to see. This will help me so much; my goal is to find a solution for Lisa."

Michelle agreed to try to get some of the information by staying after hours some night to look into the files. She was not gung-ho about doing this, but she wanted to do the right thing. Ross thanked her and took her by the hands. Their touch felt good to both of them. Ross handed a card to Michelle after putting his home phone number on the back,

"Please call me anytime, even if you just want to see a movie." She smiled.

On their way out, they ran into Arnie Doubleday. Arnie's handshake caused Michelle to feel uncomfortable, as if she had done something terribly wrong. In a way, this could be a death sentence for a good job she'd had for five years.

Michelle was really freaking out in the parking lot, so Ross told her not to worry.

"But," she replied, "he was watching us. I saw him sitting at the bar."

She drove out of the parking lot, noticing Arnie on his cell phone, most assuredly calling Allen Sharpe.

The next day Allen called Michelle into his office, and an argument ensued, with Michelle telling Sharpe he would not tell her who she could or could not see outside the office. Allen emphasized how important loyalty was to him. She didn't like the tone of his voice. She thought that Allen might have more character flaws than she originally thought.

An unexpected visit by the police to Allen's office made Michelle feel very uncomfortable. The cops stayed for about 20 minutes, making her very suspicious. She heard Allen mention to the detectives something about a Sunday night voicemail message and the Monday morning phone call with Glenn. She also heard him deny that he ever drove to the Clarksville motel.

17

Mary Redman called the office saying that she would be half an hour late.

"Late for what? I don't have her down on the calendar," Michelle thought.

At the same time, she decided that this would be a good time to stay late at the office to copy papers for Ross. Ross had called Michelle at the office, asking her out for pizza. She told him, "Well, I will be staying late at work tonight, but after I get off, I'd love to see you."

When Mary came into the office at 4:45, she and Allen left immediately. At 5:00, Michelle locked the doors to work on various projects that had piled up. She finished this about 7:30, then made her way back to the file room.

She put the work away, then took out the Chance files. Just as she was starting to copy the information, someone entered the office door. Michelle hoped that it was only the cleaning company, but after hearing the door open with keys clinking and Allen's voice, she quickly hid. Allen said to Mary, "Let me take you on a tour of the office."

"If he catches me, it's the end," Michelle thought. She decided to stay put, praying that Allen wouldn't take Mary to the file room, which was also the storage area for promotional items. She heard every word: "These are pictures of our clients." Mary, noticing a picture of Michelle, commented on her being so pretty. Allen, "Yeah, she's very sexy, but not too smart upstairs." Mary pointed to Allen in race car attire sitting in a driver's seat with a big smile.

"Yeah, I love to drive fast, live a fun life, and help my clients do the same."

"Please don't let Trevor drive fast, he's my only child."

"Heck, we'll get him a driver if you want."

She seemed amused. Allen continued:

"I have many passions, Mary, racing is just one. And you can be assured I will take good care of Trevor. What are *your* passions?"

"I'm still trying to find that passion thing, you know I never had a chance to see much. I came from a small town, married a white guy, so we stayed under the radar most of the time by staying home."

Allen really wanted to stay away from talking about Trevor or Mary's personal life. He felt it might keep her from relaxing. Allen hoped to bag and tag her if she showed any signs of being attracted to him.

The tour went into Allen's office, where the decor was black and silver with hints of gold. He pointed out the first million-dollar contract that he negotiated, bragging about his money-making abilities, saying, "This will be chump change to Trevor."

They sat down and Allen continued the sales pitch:

"Mary, I want to thank you for coming. I just want you to understand what I do and why I do it."

"What about football?"

"Oh, we did some representation with football players, but we thought it was too restrictive with salary caps and how much money they would be able to make. Even if the money is guaranteed, they still have to make the team to collect. In baseball, guaranteed money is just that; you get hurt, you don't make the team, you become a junkie - oh, that sounds so bad, sorry Mary - you still get paid in the game of baseball. That's what we are all about. In baseball,the union and agents are running the game, just the opposite than in most sports. Listen to me, Mary: money is power, it controls everyone around you, it controls who calls you back and who doesn't."

"I can see you spent some money on this room. How much for the sofa?"

"Well sit on it, it's the finest leather from Italy. Once you sit on it you will want to lay down and stretch out."

Allen made a small cough, saying, "Let's take a look at my favorite room, the video room."

On the way they stopped in the kitchen.

Mary peeked in and said "Wow."

"Yes, Mary, it's all about the wow factor."

"You even have a kitchen! Oh, how I love to cook," Mary said.

Allen hurried to uncork a bottle of Dom Perignon, pouring two glasses for a toast, "To a long, fun and money-making relationship."

When Allen took Mary into the video room, she was very impressed. It had six swivel captain chairs. It was a small room but very theater-like. Allen said, "Here, take the remote control, turn it on. It has an amazing sound system. Hit the DVD button, and you'll probably see our promotional advertisement. I've got to head to the bathroom. Oh, I haven't showed you that yet." They laughed.

Mary hit the power button and the screen came on. The picture was 80 inches, big enough to make you feel like you were at a real theater. The sounds were not of regular music or of an advertisement, but that of an X-rated movie. Allen ran into the room as he pulled up his zipper.

"Oh, I'm so sorry, Mary, one of my players must have watched something without changing the DVD. I hope it didn't upset you."

Mary seemed unfazed and simply smiled.

"Allen, why don't you keep it on?"

Allen thought to himself "This is working out just like I hoped."

He smiled back.

"Okay, before I do that, how about if I freshen up your champagne glass?"

"That would be nice."

Allen reached over Mary as both were sitting in the leather captain chairs. Just as he did so he inhaled Mary's scented hair.

He felt a shake of her body, as if a chill had run up her spine. However, with the shake came a purr, like that of a kitten being stroked.

Allen stayed there for a couple of seconds, then he pulled away the remote. Just as he did this, Mary made a move towards his lips, embracing him in a long passionate kiss.

They pulled away with a high school childish gleam of *"Oh, what did I do, let's do it again."*

Meanwhile, the screen showed two beautiful Russian ladies with a well-built and apparently well-hung actor, and they were getting very busy.

As they played footsies, Allen nodded to the screen and asked, "Have you ever tried that?"

Mary said, "Yeah, right, this country girl only knows one position and never goes experimenting. What about you?"

"Oh, no, one lady has always been enough for me," as he leaned over for another passionate kiss without any resistance. He was now in the driver's seat, as Mary said, "Yeah, one man is enough for me too."

Allen took his foot, moving it up Mary's leg, as she touched his neck while massaging his ear. Allen's large toe was making Mary wiggle a little, and her hand made a move towards his zipper. The porn was now live in the swivel seats.

Allen had Mary in his chair, his trousers down to his ankles, her plump breasts in his face. Then she got on her knees to please. She was really letting go now, alternating between giving him head and sipping her champagne. She checked his face to see if he was enjoying her talents. When Allen was completely firm, she climbed back up to straddle him. Their eyes focused together as they shifted into high gear, exchanging sounds of ecstasy.

Michelle, still hidden and forced to listen to this display, was by now steaming mad, knowing that Allen was taking advantage of Mary.

Their sexual frenzy came to an earth-shattering end, with both of them reaching climax as if they'd been waiting for this for years. Mary actually had, but for Allen it was just part of the game. A quiet aftermath of gathering emotions and clothes occurred, as Mary headed to the washroom and Allen to his office.

Michelle stayed quiet until they left. Looking at the clock, she realized that Ross had been waiting for over an hour. She hurried to finish the copying.

What a story she had to tell.

Ross was just about to leave when Michelle pulled up to the restaurant. She hurried in and gave Ross a big hug.

"Slow down, Michelle, I'm not going anywhere."

"Boy, do I have a story to tell you. You asked me to stay late to get some information for you, so I did. Then I went into the file room to get the Chance files, which I copied and brought."

"Michelle, that is great. Wow, I never thought you'd bring me the whole file."

"Ross there's more. While copying the file I heard the door open, it was Allen with Mary Redman. I couldn't believe it. He said, 'Let's go on a tour of the office,' but they never got past the video room. When Allen went to the bathroom, he gave Mary the remote control, she accidentally put on a porno. Well, when he came back, he apologized, but Mary said, 'Oh, I thought that was one of your clients performing.' Allen said, 'Should I turn it off?' Mary said, 'No, I never saw one before, so leave it on.' Before long, they were making their own porn. After she left, Allen called Arnie, telling him, 'Hey, we got the kid. I just bagged and tagged Mary, the kid is all ours.'"

Ross was speechless.

Michelle continued: "I left my umbrella in the file room, and if Allen finds it, he might wonder how it got in there."

"Get in early tomorrow, that's all you have to do."

"Okay."

"Now, let's have that beer and pizza."

"If Allen signs the kid, he will make a lot of money and try to steal it all."

"Not if I can help it."

"Allen is leaving for the Dominican Republic next week to see a 16-year-old shortstop, hoping to get a 2-million-dollar bonus for signing him. Allen will try to take 50% of that."

"Michelle, that's what I want to do: follow him around when he is there, be at the field when he is there, be at the restaurants when he is. I want to be in his jock strap."

"Oh, that's a terrible place to be, Ross."

They both laughed.

As they ate pizza, Ross looked at the Chance investment papers. He saw that Glenn was involved in many deals; with this added information, the stakes were getting higher and more dangerous for Sharpe.

There was plenty to go over. Now they needed to retain a good corporate attorney. Ross saw that Allen and his crew were all listed as general partners of the real estate investments, taking huge profits for themselves, but giving their clients nothing. A shell game and not one on Siesta Beach.

After they finished the last piece of pizza, Ross suggested that they go for a chocolate sundae. Michelle liked Ross's style. She thought, "He's perfect for me. He's smart and likes chocolate." They said goodnight. Michelle gave Ross her cell number, instructing Ross not to call the office. She also told him that the police had stopped by to see Allen.

"Ross, I'm getting a little scared of what is happening."

"Don't worry, Michelle, I'm here for you. We should have Sharpe's ass in court soon. It's a good thing the police came by. I wish I had a police report of the night Glenn killed himself. I heard from the Motel 6 people that a guy who looked like Allen had gone into the room after Glenn's death."

"Oh, Ross, I heard him yelling at Glenn on the phone. I never heard Allen so mad."

The next day, Michelle got to work early. As she went into the office, Allen was leaving the video room, holding two empty champagne glasses. He had seen her umbrella and confronted her about why it was in such a place. Michelle was freaking out, but she did her best to dodge the subject, offering to help him in the video room, but Allen quickly said, "No, thanks." Allen told Michelle to "Call Mary Redman and ask her if she enjoyed last night."

"I'm sure she did."

"Get me everything for my trip to the Dominican Republic, book the room in Costa Rica for next month, then file the citizenship papers for the kid who defected from Cuba."

18

Ross, in the meantime, got his itinerary ready for the trip. He also held meetings with his accounting firm and the lawyers, who could make sense of the legal shenanigans of the various deals. Ross suspected criminal, fraudulent, and fiduciary crimes, plus other offenses by the Sharpe group.

Agents, Ross believed, should have an ethical, moral responsibility in all client matters, especially when investing money. If Allen was found guilty of fraud, then Lisa could recover all the money that the Sharpe group had scammed from them.

Ross arrived at the international terminal, seeing Arnie and Allen sitting at the airport bar. Since Ross was flying in coach, he boarded after business class. Allen noticed Ross making his way to the back, where Arnie was sitting only three rows in front of him. Ross said to him, "You have to sit in the cheap seats without your boss?"

Ross was feeling really good now as he was stalking the agent, and the battle of right vs. wrong had shifted into high gear. As soon as the seatbelt sign was turned off, Arnie disappeared behind the curtain that separated business from economy class.

Ross studied the itinerary for his trip. He'd never traveled out of the country before and spoke little Spanish. To stay on path with Allen would be a challenge, but Michelle had helped him locate some of the destinations to be covered by Allen's three-day hunt for young baseball talent. The plane landed in Haiti, but only for a few minutes. Ross was impressed with the hundreds of people who were there just to see planes come and go.

When Ross remarked on it, the flight attendant said, "Oh, they are here every time I come, and it's always fun to see them cheer us."

Ross asked her about the Dominican Republic.

"The D.R. people have it so much better than the Haitians, not nearly the political crime and poverty. It's so sad when the people are abused by rich politicians."

"Yeah, that seems to be the case everywhere. The ruling class wants its citizens to be dumb and poor."

Once in the D.R., Ross would head to a small town known for developing great shortstops, San Pedro de Macorís. Ross took his time to debark. He was the third from last to exit the plane, already feeling the tropical humidity of Santo Domingo. capital city.

The airport was like that in a documentary of a small city in Africa. There was a strong smell of body odor, as many were wiping sweat off their brows. Competition for the American dollar was already evident, so many were trying to persuade the visitors to take a cab, a limo, a motorbike, and showing you brochures of resorts freshly built. Ross started to sweat himself as he made eye contact with Allen, who was standing next to a local guy.

Arnie arrived carrying their bags. Ross saw them move out of the terminal without going through customs. Ross, by contrast, was apprehended by two cops, who escorted him unceremoniously to a holding room.

After he identified his luggage, he was strip-searched, and his luggage was thoroughly examined.

Standing just outside the door was Allen's local contact. Ross asked who the man was, but the police acted as if they couldn't understand. However, they knew English, as English meant money.

The Dominicans are in love with America. Part of the reason is that so many kids grow up with nothing and then become millionaires overnight as baseball players. This had happened to so many young boys that the national income of the country was significantly raised by hundreds of millions of dollars that ball players brought to their country over the years. Baseball is the way out of a country that had a dim future before baseball arrived. Baseball players are raised in the D.R., the same way Kenya breeds runners, or South Korea churns out female golfers.

One of the security inspectors opened Ross' luggage, took out a baseball, then his glove, putting it on, acting like he was throwing a pitch. "Ball one," said Ross. It was clear that they were hoping to find a joint or something to hold him in jail, but they came up empty.

After hassling him for an hour or so, they finally escorted him out to the hustle of the street. Ross waved to a taxi for the ride to Punta Garza, the small resort near San Pedro de Macorís. On the way, Ross and the driver, Pedro, became comfortable with each other, talking baseball.

19

Ross really needed someone to help him around the island, especially since he spoke little Spanish and had no car. The drive was about two hours to the Punta Garza resort near San Pedro de Macorís, so Ross had time to explain to the driver, Pedro, why he came to this small town. Pedro has seen many agents, but began thinking that maybe this one was a little different.

Pedro told Ross that he had previously played baseball in the minor leagues and had once had an agent of his own. When he had a career-ending injury that sent him back to the island, his agent immediately abandoned him. Pedro had a bad taste for agents since then. Pedro's biggest regret was the girl he got pregnant in the small town of Lansing, Michigan. He told Ross that he had a daughter who was now 5 or 6, but he had no contact with her.

"Betsy was a front office girl at the age of 19 when I arrived to play ball," Pedro said. "We were hot to trot, instant attraction. Man, we had such a fight about me staying in the States, but I told Betsy that if she wanted to come live with me in the D.R., we could have a nice life. But, hell, she was told by her parents that she had better stay home. We just said goodbye and left it alone forever."

They pulled into a narrow driveway that was protected by a small gate, one that you got out to unhook. Ross was glad he had finally arrived.

"Pedro, do you always drive that fast?"

"Yeah, today I drive slow, lots of rain the last couple of days."

Ross hoped he wouldn't see the sun shine with Pedro behind the wheel. Ross checked into a room right next to the beach, a small private strip of sand. Claudia, the lady behind the desk, asked Ross if he'd like to exchange some U.S. dollars for pesos, the local currency. She explained that her exchange rate was the best, and Pedro agreed. She passed Ross the key to his bungalow, number 8.

Ross put the local currency up to his nose, taking a whiff. "This money smells like garbage, but it sure is the most colorful and prettiest money I've ever seen." Pedro walked with Ross. They stopped at the little store on the grounds, getting some water, sunscreen, and a case of beer.

"Just in case you want a beer after we go see some baseball!" Ross suggested, smiling.

"Yeah, I'll want a beer."

Ross liked this place, draped in palm trees.

"Ross, here in the D.R. you will find beauty everywhere if you take the time to see it."

Pedro told a story about a man who was being chased by a pack of dogs. He reached a cliff, looking down. As the dogs moved in on him, he decided to jump. He grabbed on to a large tree root. He looked to the root area and saw the most beautiful patch of strawberries he'd ever seen, bright red and the size of baseballs. He tasted the sweetness of the fruit.

"The moral, Ross, is that in life we have fears and death all around us, but we also have the sweetness of life everywhere. Before he ate the strawberry, he had to notice it first."

Entering his room, Ross noticed some critters that were indigenous to the beach, including a giant sand crab sitting near his pillow. Ross was startled, but Pedro picked up the hefty crab, walking it back to the water. Ross put down the broom that he was going to defend himself with, then he pulled the sheets off the bed, to see sand crabs running everywhere.

As Ross jumped back, Pedro laughed. He opened up the cabinets carefully, only to find more sand crabs. Pedro handled the extermination of the little critters, making Ross very happy to have Pedro around.

Pedro laughed, "Man, you're scared of these little bugs? We eat them."

Ross started to unpack his suitcase. Pedro peeked inside.

"You must have been in hurry to pack," he commented.

"Oh no, Pedro, you should have seen what they did to this suitcase at the airport security. Hell, they even took my baseball."

They took a walk to the beach and sat down on the pier. Ross mentioned how beautiful the ocean looked.

Pedro said, "Wait till you see the world below the water."

Ross filled Pedro in on everything from Glenn Chance to how Allen recruited players. Ross made sure that he didn't make the trip seem too vindictive or personal, but that he wanted to make his own way in the agent business, keeping young Dominican ball players from greedy agents. Pedro had heard of Enrique, the young shortstop. Ross asked Pedro if he'd go to the morning practice with him.

"Sure, we're in the same boat, my friend," Pedro said.

The workout was set up by a trainer who handled base-ball matters for Enrique. This was to showcase Enrique to some top cross-checkers, a sort of private audition to see how much money he could fetch on the open market.

The talk around the park was about two recent murders on the east side of the island involving a boat filled with Cuban baseball players. There were two American agents with a lot of cash ready to meet the boat.

Once the boat landed all hell broke loose. The Domini-can mafia told the American agents that they were repre-senting the players. A yelling match ensued, with one of the American's getting shot. This showed the high stakes behind the scenes of D.R. baseball.

Ross told Pedro that Sharpe was pressuring Enrique to sign a contract. All indications suggested that a 2-million-dollar bonus was not out of the question.

Ross explained, he was there to make sure that Enrique signed only with him. When Ross told Pedro that Allen was trying to get 50% of the kid's signing bonus, Pedro got very upset.

"Hey, that's the kid's money. When I played, we got no big money. I'm not jealous, but hey, this guy, who never caught a ground ball or took years of hitting practice, is a shithead. I want to help the kid the same way you do, Ross. I will help you."

Enrique's family knew that mucho dinero was about to be offered. They had kept all scouts away from him. Agents were getting to the kids before the scouts were, demanding big money on the open market. The agents hire local train-ers, who have a network like the cartels in Mexico.

It really becomes who finds the talent before the next guy.

"Pedro, tomorrow the kid is working out at the big park. Let's be there at 9:00 AM."

Pedro decided to take Ross out for some pollo fritta, papas frittas, and cervezas with salsa music. The restaurant was so loud that you had to point to the menu for what you wanted to eat. Ross liked the big bottle of El Presidente beer in a green bottle.

On the way back to Punta Garza, they couldn't believe what they saw – a horse standing in the middle of the road. Pedro stopped, got out, and took the rope from the neck of the horse. A small shack of a home was nearby, with a small dangling light bulb that gave enough light for Ross to say, "Knock on their door, see if they own the horse."

Pedro tapped on the door.

A very old lady opened the door, chewing a piece of bread. He asked her if this was her horse, and she shut the door quickly without saying anything. They laughed it off. Ross acted like he was going to mount the horse, but instead, they tied the horse to the tree in the front yard. Dropping Ross off at Punta Garza, they agreed to meet at 8:00 AM.

20

Morning comes pleasantly to this part of the world. Birds chirp, tides slap the shores, roosters claim their territory, palms trees sway, and flowers lie on the ground after the night winds break them free. The coffee brewed in the front office was fresh and locally grown. The owner of the Punta Garza resort also owned the baseball team. Which explained why some players (as well as baseball executives and agents) lived there during the winter ball season.

The owner, Mr. Torrez, who ran many businesses in the D.R., was a man of power and wealth. He also provided protection for the players if they got stopped by a cop for a shakedown. It was the cops' way of strong-arming the weak, but when you knew Mr. Torrez you had power,. You couldn't be extorted for money if you knew the king.

Even though baseball season was just about to start, this trip was all about getting the young players before the scouts got to them. Claudia poured Ross a cup of coffee as they chatted about baseball, then commented on his new friendship with Pedro. Ross was comforted that she had good things to say about Pedro.

When Ross headed to the beach after two cups of coffee, he noticed an unusual object lying on the sand. As he got closer, he was shocked - it was the horse from last night. He could tell because the tattered rope was still around its neck. Its throat has been slit so violently that its head just tilted to one side. Ross raced back to the room, grabbed his gear, and waited by the road. When Pedro drove up, Ross jumped in.

Pedro asked, "What did you see, a ghost?"

"You're damn right, the horse from last night was lying on the beach with its throat cut."

Pedro explained that people in the D.R. are very superstitious, with black and white magic still being practiced on the island.

"Next time we leave all the horses we find right where we find them. I don't want that to be me lying on the beach."

Their drive went through the small town of San Pedro, and Ross recognized the restaurant where they ate the night before. The area was busy with vendors setting up shop and horse carriages ready for a hopefully successful day. It would be hot today, but the slight increase of elevation at the ball field reduced some of the heat. Pedro hit his brakes, making a sharp left turn into the parking lot, which had six cars already there.

Tonight there would be a game, an exhibition game with current and former pros, that should draw about 6,000 fans, but now it was all about Enrique. The sweet smell from the upland trees gave fragrance to the park, but a sound all too familiar came from the inside—crack, bam, it was batting practice for Enrique. Great players generate a unique sound when their bat hits the ball.

They made their way up the ramp, seeing empty El Presidente beer cups and stray dogs feasting on chicken bones. The previous night's game lasted into the 13th inning, with fans getting their money's worth as the $1.00 bleacher seats were sold out.

Standing on the first base side, Ross noticed Allen's group across the field from him. He recognized one of them from the airport, but all eyes were on the hard-hit balls coming from the batting cage. The 6'3", 200-pound shortstop was showing off. On occasion he put one over the railroad tracks beyond the 365-foot sign in left field.

Ross said, "I've never seen railroad tracks in the outfield before."

"That's why we are such good fielders, our ballparks are obstacle courses," Pedro joked.

When Enrique finished hitting, he headed to shortstop. His dad went to first base.

As Enrique fielded ground balls, Sharpe walked on the field to get a closer look. So did Ross.

Sharpe pointed to Ross, sending a heavy-set guy named Carlos over, who said, "You're not allowed on the field."

Ross said, "Hey, come on man, don't treat us like that, we want to see the kid too."

Carlos said, "The kid has already signed with Sharpe. We like Sharpe because he speaks one word of Spanish, 'dinero.'"

Pedro barked back, "I know the game, not just the baseball game, we don't move for nobody."

Ross stared at Sharpe making a move towards him and the fungo hitter took a break to watch what was happening.

All of a sudden, Allen said, "You're not welcome!"

Ross said, "Move me."

They made a move towards each other.

Allen said, "How the hell did you know to be here? Was it Michelle who told you?"

"Leave her out of this, she has nothing to do with me!"

"Bullshit, I know it's Michelle. You're on the same flight, the same hotel, and the same places I'm at. That bitch is fired! Her ass is gone!"

Ross moved even closer to Allen but Pedro grabbed his arm, pulling him back. Ross moved away without going to blows. Allen yelled at Ross that the kid was already signed, and it was time to leave Enrique alone.

Ross yelled back, "The kid doesn't know what he's got himself into."

"Say that shit walking, now get out of here," Sharpe yelled.

Fielding a ball in the hole, Enrique threw a bullet to first base. Ross could see that with a talent like that, if a scout didn't sign him first, he would be able to demand millions as a free agent.

Because Michelle had given Ross the exact itinerary, they knew where Enrique lived, so they headed to his house to wait for him.

His small town was locally known as the black hole. Average pay for a hardworking man was $95 a month. A few minutes after they arrived, a blue LTD showed up, with Allen and Enrique opening the doors. Ross stood next to the dirt driveway. Allen was shocked that Ross was at Enrique's home and the two again exchanged angry words.

This small yellow wood-framed house had never seen so much action by two Americans. Allen came at Ross, but Ross kicked him in the balls, dropping him to the ground. A mule came over, making a honking sound, and pissed on Allen's leg, as Enrique laughed out loud.

Ross finally got his chance to tell Enrique that he should be careful with this agent.

Enrique was sort of shell-shocked, saying, "I'm sorry, sir, but I've already signed with him," pointing to a wet and defeated Sharpe.

"OK, don't let him steal your money, believe me that all he wants, he's a crook."

They headed back to Punta Garza. Tomorrow was his last day, and Ross wanted to go back to see Enrique.

Pedro said, "It's better we leave that alone."

"You're right, but when that kid gets to the states, I'll be all over him like seams on a baseball."

Pedro drove Ross to the airport in a heavy rain. Just over the rolling green mountains the sun was ready to dry up the short morning sprinkling that keeps this country so beautiful. At the airport Ross noticed Allen with his local buddies, more than before since now they knew he was representing Enrique. He was spreading around money to his local help. Ross took his time to get on the plane, passing Allen as they made eye contact.

While Ross didn't get to sign Enrique, he felt the trip was extremely productive. He knew he had lost the battle but would win the war. He would prove that Sharpe was a criminal and ran a corrupt sports business. Even though Allen had signed Enrique, Ross was confident that he later would come on board with him, once he had all his ducks in order to blow Allen out of the water.

Ross was happy to see Michelle, then he talked with the lawyers and accountants who had been delving into the investment documents. Lisa could be the first of a big class action lawsuit, since so many of the younger, more naïve ball players knew nothing of the investments and had been too trusting of Sharpe.

They could have a claim, since, as in most legal matters, it is the discovery of the misrepresentation that can extend the normal statute of limitations. The fiduciary responsibilities were a monster strike against Sharpe, as self-dealing could be a fraudulent activity and not registered with the S.E.C.

Lisa was ready to fight. On Ross's recommendation, Lisa hired the additional law firm of Lee and Patterson to represent her in the civil trial. Ross had said that a good attorney could get this done within a short time.

That firm hired its own accountant to work with Mark Fingers, putting together a strong case for Lisa.

The accounting disclosed investments being made in a way that showed Sharpe taking money from his clients that he then invested in his own land deals, also skimming money for management fees. Sharpe's group was the land owners, the general partners, the developers, and the property managers. It was not ethical for Sharpe to be wearing that many hats.

Investments also indicated that Sharpe had used his power of attorney privilege to withdraw money from Glenn's account, which Allen then invested in a Wyoming gold mine. Lisa was asked by the law firm about what dialogue she had with Sharpe after Glenn's death. She responded that there had been none.

Sharpe had ignored her and was completely unresponsive. Further investigation showed Sharpe had put himself down as the beneficiary on two of Glenn's life insurance policies. It was Lisa who had initiated these insurance contracts. It would be obvious in court that Glenn never would have asked for the beneficiary to be in Sharpe's name.

21

Lisa by this time had built up a friendship with Michelle. One evening Lisa and Michelle were out having dinner, when a note was sent to their table. They thought it was a note from an admirer, offering to buy them a drink. Michelle opened the folded bar napkin.

The note said: "We're watching every move you make. Keep it up and it will be your last move."

Lisa asked the waitress who sent this note. She pointed to a Mexican busboy.

Lisa approached him and said, "Tell me who gave you this piece of paper."

The Mexican boy said, "No speak English," as he pointed to the bar.

Lisa went back to Michelle suggesting that it must have been the two men who were staring at them. Michelle called Ross, who showed up ten minutes later.

Ross was greeted with a hug from Michelle. It was clear that they had desperately missed each other. Michelle filled him in on what had happened earlier. Ross approached the bus boy, but he got nowhere in his questioning. The waitress came over and said that the bartender saw a heavy-set man give Jose the note.

"It had to be Arnie," Michelle said.

Ross decided it would best to go on record, so they called the police.

The police dismissed it as a prank, but Ross took the napkin and taped it to his car dashboard.

Lisa said to Ross, "They won't stop me. Yes, I'm a little frightened, but I'm more determined than ever."

Michelle took a day off from work. She was certain that this would end badly for her. Ross told her, "Quit, just quit! You can come work for me."

Michelle told Ross that she had never quit a job and that being fired was better than being a quitter. When Michelle went back to work, she found that the door locks had been changed. She was shocked by this and called Ross.

He told her, "Okay, Michelle, I'll meet you at Krispy Kreme in ten."

Michelle left a note on the office door asking Allen to call her immediately.

When Michelle got back home, there was a message on her answering machine: "Hey, Michelle, this is Arnie. How was dinner at Applebee's with Lisa? How about the donuts at Krispy Kreme? It's nice you're home so early."

Michelle was scared out of her mind. Ross came and listened to the message.

He told her, "Take the tape out, we need this as evidence. What a classless asshole!"

"But, Ross, what if they want to hurt me?"

"Don't worry, I've got you covered."

Lisa received some strange phone calls as well, the type where no one spoke when she answered.

Lisa was grilled by her attorneys. They had to know everything now. It was crunch time. There was plenty of hard evidence to go after Allen, but the attorneys must be right; nothing could go wrong.

They asked her, "Did you and Glenn love each other? Were you and Glenn about to get a divorce? Did Glenn have another lover?"

Lisa said, "No, everything was fine with us. He was just sad about the IRS, and he felt bad about trusting his agent. The IRS investigation put him into a deep depression."

Michelle was grilled the same way, "Did you ever have an affair with Allen? Did you sleep with any of Allen's clients to get them to sign on with his company? Did you return the Chance documents to the file room after you copied them?"

"I only copied them."

Michelle was getting very upset, but the attorneys said, "We have to hammer you, as this might come up in court. We need to be prepared on all fronts. It's only part of our strategy." Michelle said, "Wait, I left out something. I did sleep with Allen one time, a mistake. Please don't tell Ross."

The attorneys agreed, "We won't, but it's best we know, so if it comes up, we can face the facts."

Michelle went back to work to clean out her desk. Before she even got into the office, Allen met her at the door. He grabbed her arm, shoving her into the umbrella rack.

Then he pleaded with her, "We once were so close. We have spent 5 years together."

"Not any more, leave me alone."

Michelle pulled herself up.

Allen was panicked. He thought, "What have I done?" He knew his days were numbered. His attempt to reconcile was fruitless, but he tried one last-ditch effort.

"If you say anything, you're dead."

Michelle fled. When she got home, she immediately called Ross, who hurried over to her apartment. She told him what happened at the office.

"I was just going to get my things and leave him a note, but it seemed like he was waiting for me. I was so scared. He grabbed me and threw me down. He said he would kill me." Ross hugged her and assured her that he would always protect her.

She melted into his hug, feeling relieved as they held each other.

22

Lee and Patterson filed the lawsuit, with papers being served at Sharpe's Peoria office on a day he was present to receive them. The complaint included counts on behalf of Lisa Chance for misrepresentation, illegal use of funds, internal self-dealing, fiduciary impropriety, SEC violations, with other counts. The lawsuit would be tried in the State of Illinois. The legal team had an additional ace in the hole: Allen had tampered with evidence at a crime scene. That was yet another matter.

Allen was prepared to fight, but he pursued an easier way out. He made a call to Ross requesting a meeting.

Ross responded, "We can meet in court!"

The attorneys set up a good strategy for the trial - have the room filled with former clients who were upset with Sharpe, having been treated unfairly by him, including Mrs. Redman, plus others who wanted their money back.

Lisa's testimony would be key. Without her involvement, this could not have happened. Most clients sign away all their rights, entering into agreements of confidentiality, with hold-harmless clauses.

Sharpe had trust accounts, power of attorney privileges and his wife even owned life insurance policies on many clients with Sharpe being the beneficiary.

Accounting showed players paying back losses due to bad advice, a tax issue called 776 transactions, where the general partner can buy back from the original investor after depreciation. It was another nail in Sharpe's legal coffin.

Papers showed how Allen missed many tax advantages for his players, covering them up so he would not have to pay them back for the mistakes he made. The poor athletes were getting double-taxed and paying 5% for management fees to the Sharpe group. Over-inflated phantom income was losing the tax write-offs. There was so much evidence, Sharpe not only stood to lose his fortune, he also could go to prison.

In order to make a slam dunk case, the proof would have to be a little more obvious to the court, with subpoenaed canceled checks proving Sharpe had a special account where he drew money from clients' bank accounts with his power of attorney. This could prove to be more damaging than all the other finds. After further calculation and with meticulously detailed planning, another letter was sent to Sharpe on behalf of former clients who demanded retribution and recovery. Not surprisingly, Sharpe ignored it.

Lee and Patterson staged a mock trial in a special courtroom they built. They needed to practice as if before a big game. They felt that this would help them get the bugs out before a big win. They hired another firm, supplied with details of the case, to be an opposing firm to practice with for two days of intense courtroom procedures. They were as confident as Steve Carlton was in a game that had to be won.

Former clients were asked to appear in court. This might help the judge make the best decision after seeing their anguished faces. Depositions were taken and most of the former players were eager to cooperate with Lee and Patterson. The clients never knew to ask Sharpe about tactics such as phantom income, suspended losses, and passive carry-overs. They were too busy hitting a hard-breaking slider or creating movement on a fastball.

Athletes were such easy victims for those who preyed on them. Sharpe's company needed to dig a deep hole and hide, but there would be no hiding from these crimes. Sharpe's ego told him this couldn't be happening; he was the king of the hill. People simply did whatever he told them to do - he owned them. Sharpe knew that the only way out was to fight.

This action could also reveal that the players' association was well aware of the criminal nature of the Sharpe group and other agents. This was a big deal.

Rarely are agents taken to court, charged with neglect of fiduciary responsibilities, and other violations. There's a reason why so many of these cases are hidden under the rug - the players' association was very good at keeping these issues media-quiet.

They knew that if bad press got out about agents stealing from the players, it would weaken the power of the players' association, and soon the owners would have the upper hand. The union knew very well that the various agents controlled the players and the big money.

Ross was considering doing a complete investigation of the players' association's history of dealing with disgruntled players who had been victimized by their agents. He would look into MLBPA's handling of agent disputes and advising players on financial matters.

Ross was now in charge of bringing down one of base-ball's biggest agents. It was time for him to make a name for himself in the game of baseball...this time off the field.

Who was running baseball, anyway? It wasn't the play-ers. The players seemed to be puppets of the agents, obey-ing them the way they obeyed their Little League coaches. Agents ran baseball, manipulating teams with this player or that player.

They got deals closed that never should have been done, telling owners, "It's my guy and I control him."

If Sharpe was found guilty, agents would be viewed dif-ferently, not only by the players but by the fans as well. Owners would certainly like it.

The way to win in labor disputes is to win the fans to your side.

23

The scene at the courthouse was chaotic. Not only were there hundreds of media cameras, but hundreds of baseball fans too, some even surging forward to try and get autographs. Ross, Lisa and Michelle, and other clients who were once with the Sharpe group entered the courthouse. Camera crews were begging for interviews; however Ross asked everyone to refrain from talking to the press. He told the media they would talk to them after they won the verdict.

The players, for their part, hoped to find out something about their own investments. This could lead to a class action suit bankrupting Sharpe. The media feeds on this sort of news, like sharks that get into a frenzy when bloody chum is thrown overboard.

Once seated in the courtroom, the players, families, owners, and media waited with high expectations. Allen was with his support group...the ass-kissers. However, the primary focus was all about Sharpe. He sat next to his attorney, while his retinue of cronies sat directly behind him, all wearing polo shirts. After everyone was sworn in by Judge Williams, you could feel the pressure heating up.

Mrs. Redman was sitting with Trevor, whose arm was in a sling from an on-field brawl in his first game as a pro. Michelle sat on the other side of Mary Redman, who remembered the night that Sharpe took advantage of her.

Ross sat next to Mark Fingers with the trial lawyers. Mark had some very damaging information he was able to obtain during three days of visiting Sharpe's Beverly Hills office.

The criminal investigation surrounding Glenn's death was complete. A fingerprint was taken from the flushing handle of the Motel 6 toilet. Sharpe was directly linked to being in the room on the day of the suicide.

The once mighty sports agent was about to go down. Civil law was still powerful. The statute of limitations was still in effect, since the time of discovery trumped the long years that had passed. A big class action lawsuit by all his former clients was very possible.

Representing Sharpe was a lady in a red dress, red lipstick, and red hair - a pit bull with lipstick. Her red appearance gave off a sense of fire, a statement of power and persuasion without offering a word. She had put the tail between the legs of many opposing lawyers, who easily got intimidated. She was Monica Cheeks, in her early 50s, who had made a name for herself since starting private practice over 15 years ago. The charges against her client included: negligence, gross negligence, aiding and abetting fraud, breach of fiduciary duty, misrepresentation of limited partnerships, and violation of SEC provisions.

Wayne Patterson was going to be asking the questions throughout the trial on behalf of Lisa. The first person to take the witness stand was Mark Fingers. He was asked if he had visited Allen Sharpe's Beverly Hills office.

FINGERS: "Yes, my first thought was whether Sharpe joined the office buildings together so he could collect rent from the expensive Rolls-Royce office. Heck, the name of the street was Sharpe Lane. The place stank of self-dealing and greed. All I wanted to do was look at the books, see who was paying rent, see if Glenn had invested in the buildings, and, if so, how much money should be coming back to his bank account, since Glenn never received a penny on his investments. I wanted the agreements of the various tenants who were paying rent. They kept telling me the records were in another location. I knew then that they were hiding something."

PATTERSON: "How long did you stay looking at the books?"

FINGERS: "I planned to stay 2 days, but I had to stay one day longer, as it was difficult to get the information I needed. Once I got some of the prospectuses, I was in business. The thing is, I waited until the Sharpe brothers left the office, then I asked the secretary to see the books. That's when I struck oil. They thought they were bullet-proof until then. I found the brothers were General Partners in the investments. They were buying back the partnerships from the clients in transactions that showed losses, but there would be great returns later. I needed to find out about passive gains, carry forwards and carried losses. Glenn was in four major investments. I found out that the land, partly owned by Glenn, was not receiving any income, as the General Partners were giving themselves giant salaries for running the business. Smoking guns for sure. I was getting all the information I needed by only flipping through a few pages of those prospectuses. The General Partners (the Sharpes) were even cutting down the trees and selling them to lumber companies with no disclosure. The game was a shell game, making things very difficult to track. These guys could doctor up anything, so a ball player couldn't understand what was going on."

PATTERSON: "What do you look for tracking this type of money?"

FINGERS: "It's all in chasing the paper trails left behind and tracing it back to where it all started. I guess maybe the guys would have never given me the books, but when Ruth gave them to me, I knew I could figure it out. All it took was one flip to page 23, and I saw the name of a holding company and it was directly attached to the Sharpe group. They were the General Partners in the deals that their clients were investing in, which is against SEC regulations. When I arrived at their office, it was very cordial with "How are you, Mark, and I know a very good restaurant," but after a while I knew what was behind the bullshit. It was the old saying, keep your friends close, but your enemies even closer. I informed the attorneys that the K-l's, which were a schedule of the investments, were incorrect, and allocation of debt was mapped out to show Glenn's vulnerability."

The visit to the Sharpe office took place at their office headquarters in Beverly Hills. Mark talked more about how they showed him around to the various offices, bragging like an overconfident athlete, the arrogance was appalling. There were many companies renting space in their office complex.

FINGERS: "I asked many times to see the lease agreements from Mercedes-Benz, Harley Davidson, Rolex and the others who had their names on the doors. Allen would always reply we can get to that later."

Mark explained the need to have these revealing leases, since Glenn was part-owner of the office complex, and any income from rent was part of the income owed to him. He elaborated that Glenn was persuaded to invest in the real estate investments that Sharpe promised would yield big dividends. Mark explained that he never got the leases, and once he left to put together Chance's financial portfolio, he was denied the valuable documents to show the nature of the investments. Fingers described the shell game of investments as similar to pinning the tail on the donkey. He showed on a chart why the investments were hard to follow, as tax shelters usually are.

FINGERS: "The chart showed the first years of the money invested by Glenn at the time of the investments. I could see the charts were off. Hell, they even had a trust account without the Chances even knowing about it. Naturally, Allen having the power of attorney provided secrecy."

He confirmed that the attorneys had issued subpoenas to obtain all of these Sharpe documents. Glenn had no chance of knowing that information, since Sharpe asked Glenn to sign real estate contracts on the last day of every year without reviewing the prospectuses. Mark told the court this was very clever of Allen and that Glenn, trusting his representatives, made it easy for him not to question the purpose of writing big checks to the one he trusted so much. If he had had an expert examine the deals, he would have known that his agents were getting a cut from all investments as General Partners, taking fees for everything, even selling timber for personal profit from the land that the players invested in.

Lisa Chance was next to tell her story, and Monica, during cross-examination, tried her best to paint an ugly landscape of the marriage.

MONICA: "Lisa, did Glenn have many ladies whom he used for sex? Was his baseball personality very temperamental?"

LISA: "Are you trying to insinuate Glenn killed himself because of some fabricated questions like that? Glenn and I had some rocky times, but I'm sure you do as well, right, Miss Cheeks?"

MONICA: "I can't say, I have never been married."

LISA: "Besides, if every woman left her boyfriend or husband for indiscretions with the other sex, no one would be living with anyone. Anyways, he was faithful to me. Our big issues were due to our finances. I was angry at Glenn for trusting his agent so much. He always said we had to trust them. They always said in the end, we will have more money than what we would have made playing ball, but I never felt that way. I guess Glenn looked up to them, sort of admiring the sophistication of very intelligent men, especially while being surrounded by tobacco-chewing locker room teammates."

MONICA: "Did Glenn have depression, Mrs. Chance? It was known his baseball career ended without him really achieving what he hoped to achieve."

LISA: "No matter how hard you try to make this look like Glenn had demons from our marriage or his baseball days, that is just a joke. His real sadness came from trusting Sharpe company.

MONICA: "Did Glenn seem upset before he checked into the Motel 6?"

LISA: "I didn't know that he had checked into Motel 6. What made Glenn really upset was when he called Allen, and he didn't get return phone calls. Glenn knew he was in a mess, but how could he figure it out? The IRS and tax liability, he just needed to find out, he wanted help. He always questioned whether he really owed that much money, but he had no one to help him. His heart was broken when Allen turned his back on him."

Monica Cheeks had clearly lost this battle, and Lisa was dismissed. Patterson next requested Allen Sharpe to take his oath, calling him as a hostile witness. He was prepared like Ted Williams was on a 3 & 1 fastball, ready to rip him apart.

PATTERSON: "So, Allen, when did you meet Glenn?"

ALLEN: "During his short rookie season in 1976."

PATTERSON: "When did he agree to have you and your firm represent him?"

ALLEN: "During that short rookie season."

PATTERSON: "Let's get down to the nuts and bolts of this case, Mr. Sharpe. When did you start investing money from Glenn?"

ALLEN: "It was after he visited us at our office and saw the first million-dollar certificate I had hanging on the wall of my office."

PATTERSON: "When Glenn was attracted to investing with you, did you include Lisa in the picture?"

ALLEN: "No, it was Glenn playing ball, not Lisa."

PATTERSON: "You never included her, because she would be much more diligent in reviewing the investments, not falling for the great prospects of the future? Did you send prospectuses of investments for Glenn to sign on the last day of December, with pressure to sign quickly and make out checks?"

ALLEN: "Yes, that was the way we did it."

PATTERSON: "But do you think that was ample time for the Chances to look into what they were investing in?

ALLEN: "It was up to them, not me."

PATTERSON: "Mr. Sharpe, how many clients do you have?"

ALLEN: "We have 67 as of today."

PATTERSON: "After today, that number will be much lower, believe me."

Patterson pressed on:

PATTERSON: "Did you take advantage of Mrs. Redman?"

ALLEN: "Look, she was hungry for the chance to have some fun. It was obvious that after her husband died, she hit rock bottom and all the attention was being paid to Trevor instead of her. I invited her to see the office and have dinner."

PATTERSON: "That seems pretty callous and shallow. Are you an opportunist? Do you take advantage of people, Mr. Sharpe?"

ALLEN: "No more than you do."

PATTERSON: "Mr. Sharpe, what are your partnerships with the investments? I mean, do you take commissions, and is your group the General Partners in the investments you put your clients into?"

ALLEN: "Well, we feel we're entitled to do that. We put all this together, trying to make good choices for our clients."

PATTERSON: "I'm sure the SEC would have something to say about that."

Patterson continued:

PATTERSON: "Is keeping income from your clients smart business?"

ALLEN: "It is if you know the way some of the athletes waste their money."

PATTERSON: "Yes, Mr. Sharpe, we all have desires, but when those desires get fraudulent, you have to pay the price. Enough of this guy."

Michelle was then sworn in.

PATTERSON: "What was your main job at Sharpe's of-fice?"

MICHELLE: "Well, to be honest, it was putting out fires with unhappy clients."

PATTERSON: "What do you mean?"

MICHELLE: "The athletes often called to ask questions about their investments. This was very sticky for me as some of them were my friends, and I was not always so involved. I felt horrible for them, but what could I do? I couldn't bite the hand that fed me. After Mrs. Redman was manipulated to get Trevor to sign a contract, I was done with his disgusting tactics."

PATTERSON: "Whose tactics exactly?"

MICHELLE: "Sharpe, who else? These guys thought what looked good at the time or what sounded good at the time was enough. However, what looked good in one year could later be disastrous. That is what made my job so difficult. I had to clean up the mess. When I saw a once-great athlete who had millions going into a spiral financial fall, it affected me greatly."

PATTERSON: "Do you think they were cheated?"

MICHELLE: "Come on, I saw the transcripts, but I had to keep my mouth shut. I only wanted to make things manageable for the players. I knew that distributions were never sent to the players. Allen would say, let them call for the money. I wanted to help the athletes, but I had the loyalty of a soldier who believed that things would get better."

Patterson then brought Arnie Doubleday to the stand.

PATTERSON: "Mr. Doubleday, how long did you work for Mr. Sharpe?"

ARNIE: "We've been friends about 10 years."

PATTERSON: "What was your purpose in working with Sharpe?"

ARNIE: "Well, he is a big time agent, and I'm a small time insurance salesman, so he asked me to find talent on the ball field."

PATTERSON: "Were you paid?"

ARNIE: "My expenses, such as restaurants, travel and that sort of stuff."

PATTERSON: "How did you meet Mrs. Redman?"

ARNIE: "Everybody heard about Trevor, it was my job to get the kid, set up a meeting with Sharpe, and get him signed."

PATTERSON: "Under any circumstances?"

ARNIE: "Whatever it would take. Most of the time I was just being flashy when I needed to be. Heck, I'd rent a fancy car just for the day to show the kid we had class."

PATTERSON: "Did you know Michelle, who worked for Sharpe?"

ARNIE: "Yes."

PATTERSON: "Were you asked to follow her inside a mall?"

ARNIE: "No, it just happened that I was at the same place where she happened to be."

PATTERSON: "Did you hand her a note threatening her, or make a phone call to scare her? Don't forget, you're under oath."

ARNIE: "Look, Sharpe asked me on occasion to do some bad things. I was sorry for that, but he thought Michelle was getting too close to someone he felt was a threat. I never did anything illegal. Sharpe was my boss."

PATTERSON: "No more questions, we've heard enough."

24

After the trial was over and the victory against Sharpe had been secured, Ross was feeling great about how things were going. Finally, both personally and professionally, everything was moving in a positive direction, and he was basking in the good publicity from the trial. Even though Sharpe appealed the judgment to the appellate court, he had been required to post a surety bond for the full amount of the judgment. As a result, if Sharpe lost the appeal or skipped out on paying the judgment, the surety bond company would be on the hook to pay the full judgment to Lisa.

Ross ordered three dozen of reprints of the Peoria Journal Star feature article on the Sharpe civil verdict for publicity. Once he had learned all the different ways that Sharpe had used to cheat his clients, especially after the jury had readily understood the impropriety of Sharpe's greed, Ross decided that he needed to do something to help prevent the same things from happening to future players.

One of the first things that Ross did was to order a complete copy of the entire transcript of the Sharpe trial. He sent a copy of the transcript with a cover letter to both MLB and the MLBPA. He pointed out in his cover letter that what was shown at the trial was just the tip of the iceberg of what unscrupulous agents were doing to their players.

He urged both groups to adopt regulations that would apply to all agents working for players in the major leagues. He included in each letter the suggestion that, if MLB and the MLBPA failed or refused to take any such action, especially after they were now informed of the problem's existence, they also might be included in any future litigation against agents.

Ross didn't delude himself about how rough the road to agent regulation would be, but that didn't stop him. He was pleased when both MLB and the MLBPA responded to his letters informing him that the 1985 CBA already authorized the MLBPA to both investigate the problem and adopt regulations to govern player agents' activities. Due to that agreement, MLB suggested to Ross that he should direct all future communication in this regard to the MLBPA.

Once the media reported Sharpe's disorderly conduct conviction, Ross ordered reprints of the Decatur Herald-Review feature article covering the criminal charges, the guilty plea conviction, and his response. He ordered the same number of reprints as the Peoria Journal-Star article.

Ross sent this second reprint to the MLBPA. He wanted them to be aware of the level of concern that both the general public and their law enforcement representatives had about criminal behavior by players' agents, especially in Illinois.

He also enclosed a copy of MLB's letter requesting him to deal directly with the MLBPA. In his letter he asked the MLBPA to inform him what steps it was considering taking now that it was authorized to do so, what he could do to help, and when the regulations would be implemented. Ross was surprised when the MLBPA sent him a response letter inviting him to join the committee that was working on developing the proposed regulations to govern player agents.

The increased publicity from the Sharpe verdicts soon led to more work than Ross and his assistant Laura could handle. He decided to add a second full-time employee – Michelle. Laura's primary duties would be the overall office functions, while Michelle's focus would be more on Ross' outside activities, such as endorsement deals, MLBPA activities, and recruiting functions.

25

Sharpe and Monica Cheeks were in shock from the jury's verdict. Refusing to accept any blame for what happened, Allen was raging at Monica while she was packing her documents to leave the courtroom.

"How could you let this happen? I thought you said we were okay! I demand that you file an immediate appeal!"

She also told him to let her do the talking to the press.

They expected to encounter the press as soon as the courtroom doors were opened. Instead, they were greeted by uniformed police officers who told Allen he was under arrest for obstruction of justice in the death of Glenn Chance. Before Allen could say anything other than "What?" he was in handcuffs.

While Monica asked one of the officers to see the arrest warrant, two other officers led Allen past the surprised media, who immediately stuck microphones in front of him, peppering him with questions. The officers put him in a patrol car in full view of the cameras for the evening news.

Monica reviewed the arrest warrant. It showed that it had been issued by a judge in Shelbyville, Illinois, the county seat for Shelby County, in which Clarksville was located. It stated that Sharpe was arrested for violating Section 31-4(a)(1) of the Illinois Criminal Code (720 ILCS 5/ 31-4(a)(1)), for obstruction of justice by his destruction of evidence related to the death of Glenn Chance in Room 17 of the Motel 6 in Clarksville, Illinois in Shelby County on March 16, 1986.

When she asked Sergeant Woods where Sharpe was being taken, he told her to the Shelby County Jail. Checking an Illinois map, Monica took the quickest route to Shelbyville. She had no trust that Sharpe would keep his mouth shut either while being escorted to the Shelby County Jail, or after he was booked and incarcerated.

She knew that the sooner she got there, the sooner she could see him, calm him down, and keep him quiet. She called her secretary to relate to her what had happened and to tell her that she was driving straight to Shelbyville. She asked her to consult Illinois' Sullivan's Law Directory to find out who were the current Sheriff, States Attorney, full Circuit Court Judge, and the most experienced criminal defense attorneys in Shelby County.

While she waited for Sharpe to be fingerprinted, Monica called her secretary back. She was told that the Sheriff was Martin McMahon, the States Attorney was Daniel Delaney, and the full Circuit Court Judge was Donald Wilcox. She was also informed that the two most experienced criminal defense attorneys were Reginald Love and Richard Sweeney.

Monica talked to Sheriff McMahon, who then put her in touch with States Attorney Delaney. He said that Sharpe would not be released on his own recognizance, since obstruction of justice was a Class 4 felony. He didn't mention that he wasn't interested in appearing soft on crime, especially in the face of all the negative publicity surrounding the Sharpe civil trial just completed. He confirmed that Sharpe would be given a bail hearing at the courthouse at

9:00 AM tomorrow. Finally, he said that he would recommend Love instead of Sweeney.

Monica knew she had her work cut out for her as soon as she finally got to see Sharpe.

He asked angrily, "What took you so long? When are we leaving? I want you to sue the cops and the State's Attorney for false arrest, malicious prosecution, or anything else we can hit them with!"

She finally had to interrupt, marching right up to him, "Allen, sit down, shut up, stop wasting what little time we have!"

Sharpe initially resisted Monica's recommendation that an experienced local criminal defense attorney represent him in this criminal matter instead of her. She explained to him that it was not his money, but his freedom that was now at stake.

He needed someone who was an expert in criminal law and familiar with the local system. Having her handle his criminal matter instead of an experienced local criminal defense attorney would be like having a proctologist perform brain surgery. She recommended Reggie Love over Dick Sweeney.

Monica met with Reggie Love in his office in downtown Shelbyville. It was within walking distance of the historic Shelby County Courthouse.

The Courthouse, the only building in the middle of a square block, was the oldest building in town, having been completed in 1879. He thought Associate Judge Erik Davis would be the bond judge tomorrow; however Circuit Judge Donald Wilcox probably would be the trial judge.

He anticipated that Sharpe's bail would be set at a reasonable level, since it appeared to be Sharpe's first offense, and he shouldn't be considered a flight risk, especially with his sports agency and his home both being located in Illinois.

He would make arrangements tonight with a local bail bondsman to post bail, so Sharpe could return to his office right away. The bail bondsman would be present at the courthouse tomorrow with the necessary bond papers ready to be signed. He made a copy of the arrest warrant for his file, telling her he would call her tomorrow after the hearing.

The next morning Love met with Sharpe in a holding area for prisoners at the courthouse. He was humiliated after spending a night in jail. After Sharpe signed the Attorney Representation Agreement, Love filed his Appearance before the hearing. He told Sharpe to let him do all the talking, then they would meet the bail bondsman to sign the bond documents as soon as the hearing was over. The bail hearing went as Love had predicted, with Sharpe successfully posting bail.

In Love's office with the door closed, Love asked Sharpe, "Why don't you start by telling me what this is all about."

Sharpe explained that Glenn Chance was a former baseball player client of his, but that their contract had ended well over a year ago. He had been getting a succession of very desperate telephone calls from Chance over the last six months, but, since he was no longer a client, he mostly ignored them.

He got a voicemail message on Sunday night, March 15, 1986, from Chance. Around 11:00 AM the next morning, Chance called again from a Motel 6 in Clarksville, sounding extremely upset. Sharpe said he put the call on speakerphone to let Chance rant on in the background, until all of a sudden, he heard what sounded like a gunshot, then he heard nothing more. Something told him that, even if

Chance was no longer a client, he should check things out. If he did shoot himself, the Motel 6 people would have called the local police to investigate.

By the time Sharpe got to Motel 6, he saw no police presence. The desk lady told him that Chance was in Room 17, after Sharpe told her that his friend had called him, saying he needed his help. He went to Glenn's room, knocked, then went into the room. He saw that Glenn was already dead, lying stiff on the bed with the gun at his side. Since there was nothing he could do for Glenn, he decided it was best to just leave quickly. He drove straight back to Peoria.

Love asked Sharpe if there was anything else. Sharpe told him that he had received a telephone call from the Clarksville Police in the next few days, at which time he claimed to be surprised at Glenn's suicide.

He told the police that he had received a voicemail message from Glenn on Sunday night, and that he received a call late Monday morning from Glenn, but that he had hung up on Glenn after reminding him that he was no longer a client. Love asked Allen if he had touched Glenn's body. He denied doing so. Based on this discussion, he agreed that Sharpe would plead not guilty at his upcoming arraignment hearing.

Love and Sharpe were not too upset when they got together after the evidence production by the States Attorney's office. They reviewed it in Love's office after the arraignment hearing, at which Sharpe pled not guilty. Love explained to Sharpe that he was specifically charged with:

Sec. 31-4. Obstructing justice.

A person obstructs justice when, with intent to prevent the apprehension or obstruct the prosecution or defense of any person, he or she knowingly commits any of the following acts:

(1) Destroys, alters, conceals or disguises physical evidence, plants false evidence, furnishes false information;.

Love told Sharpe that the crime was a "Class 4 felony," the sentence for which was "1-3 years," with a possible extension to "3-6 years" under certain circumstances. Love further explained that the charge might be subject to possible dismissal, since the act that Glenn had committed was the act of suicide. Since Sharpe had not obstructed any person's apprehension or prosecution, Love suggested that might be a basis for dismissal of the charge.

They discussed the initial compilation of evidence against Sharpe, which included:

(1) Sharpe's driver's license photo that was identified by Amy, the desk clerk, as the male inquiring about Glenn at the front desk;

(2) phone records showing the telephone calls made from Glenn's room to Sharpe's office, both the short call on Sunday night and the longer call made late Monday morning.

(3) the fact that Amy the next day reported "a sort of burnt smell" in that room;

(4) a second examination of the Room 17 bathroom revealed a finding of a charred portion of a page behind the toilet on the floor, which contained writing excerpts that were identified by a handwriting expert to be Glenn's handwriting, but which Sharpe claimed to know nothing about;

(5) burnt paper residue was found both in the sink and, to a lesser extent, in the sink trap, and

(6) Sharpe's denial of being in Glenn's room, in spite of Amy's eyewitness identification of him and his fingerprint.

Love also explained that, at best, the evidence was circumstantial and proved nothing other than that Sharpe had been at the motel and left.

Love also discussed the possibly of a reduced charge of "disorderly conduct":

Sec. 26-1. Disorderly conduct.

(a) A person commits disorderly conduct when he or she knowingly:

(1) Does any act in such unreasonable manner as to alarm or disturb another and to provoke a breach of the peace

After explaining the various possibilities, Sharpe authorized Love to see if he could strike a plea bargain to a disorderly conduct charge, which was only a Class 3 misdemeanor with a sentence of up to 30 days, with either that sentence being suspended or Sharpe being granted probation.

Before Love even had the chance to begin negotiations with the States Attorney, the other shoe dropped. Love's office received a second batch of evidence discovery from the States Attorney's office.

Apparently, because Sharpe had never served in the armed forces or had any prior arrests, he had not undergone any prior fingerprinting. However, after he was fingerprinted in the Shelby County Jail, his prints were compared to those prints taken during the investigation of Glenn's motel room.

They were reported to be a perfect match to those taken from the room's outside doorknob, the toilet flush handle, and one of the sink faucet handles. Love was shocked when he read these documents, since they proved not only that Sharpe had done more in the room than just check on Glenn, but that he was the person who burned Glenn's documents. Love now realized that Sharpe was a lying scumbag.

Love immediately called Sharpe, ordering him to be in his office early the next morning. When Sharpe asked why, he was told, "just be here or get yourself another criminal defense attorney."

When Sharpe showed up, Love immediately went on the attack: "How stupid are you that you think it's OK to lie to your attorney, who's trying to keep your ass out of jail?"

Sharpe at first continued his denial but caved in when Love stopped him in mid-sentence, "Either shut the hell up right now and tell me what really happened inside that motel room or get your ass out of my office."

Finally, Sharpe told him that he had lied because he thought he could get away with it, since he thought he had wiped everything down.

Love then laid out his thoughts about Sharpe's remaining options. Very upset about his lying, Love was committed to representing him. In his opinion, Sharpe could kiss goodbye any previously discussed possibility of probation or a suspended sentence. Now, having Sharpe's fingerprints in the bathroom, there was no way that the States Attorney would agree to no time served.

They still had their dismissal argument that obstruction of justice didn't apply when there was no apprehension or prosecution of anyone for Glenn's suicide. If they pursued that, the risk-reward was stark – either freedom for Sharpe or a minimum one-year prison term, regardless of any potential shortening for good behavior. He wasn't even sure that the States Attorney would plea bargain down to a disorderly conduct charge, with a one-month maximum sentence to be served in the county jail.

When Love met with States Attorney Dan Delaney, he got right to the point. They had too much respect for each other to bullshit. Delaney argued that Sharpe's fingerprints in the bathroom made the case a slam dunk winner. Love responded that, even though Sharpe had been in the room, he hadn't obstructed anything because, since Glenn committed suicide, there was no culprit to apprehend or prosecute. His forthcoming motion to dismiss should be granted, leaving Sharpe a free man.

Delaney countered that Sharpe's destruction of the physical evidence included Sharpe's own apprehension or prosecution for any crime. They both recognized the lack of certainty of their positions.

Rather than take the risk of either one of them losing in a motion to dismiss hearing, they agreed that if Sharpe would plead guilty to a disorderly conduct charge - which would result in a maximum sentence of one month in the Shelby County jail - they would recommend that to the judge. Love agreed to discuss it with Sharpe.

When Love talked with Sharpe, he recommended accepting the deal. It avoided any possible felony conviction, however remote, thereby eliminating both prison time and the loss of all privileges that being a felon involves.

Instead, it would only be a misdemeanor conviction, similar to public drunkenness, a bar fight, drag racing, etc. It meant that the most time that he should actually serve would be one month, which was really no more time than a long vacation.

Finally, it meant that he would never serve time in an Illinois penitentiary, or, for that matter, in a county jail of the type in Chicago, Rockford, Peoria, Springfield, Rock Island or East St. Louis.

Historically, the Shelby County jail didn't always fill all of its cells, which could mean that Sharpe might not even share a cell all of the time.

After extended discussion, he agreed. "I guess that's what I'm paying you for."

The following Friday, Judge Donald Wilcox's courtroom was full for Sharpe's sentencing. Ross, Lisa and Michelle had gotten there early to get front row seats; many reporters were among the crowd.

Judge Wilcox accepted Sharpe's guilty plea, sentencing him to serve one month in the Shelby County Jail, to be served immediately by agreement (Sharpe wanted to "get it over").

Ross, Lisa and Michelle all smiled with relief and satisfaction to see justice served, as they looked Sharpe right in the face, while he was handcuffed and led from the courtroom by the sheriff's deputies.

26

Ross was glad to hear from the MLBPA in December that its Executive Board had issued preliminary approval of the Committee's proposed Regulations Governing Player Agents. The Board's approval meant that the MLBPA would be able to adhere to its projected timetable to have final Regulations officially adopted by mid-summer 1988.

By the end of December, the MLBPA sent a copy of the proposed Regulations to MLB for its response by January 31, 1988. On February 15th, the MLBPA submitted a set of proposed Regulations to each team for *their* response, to each of its player members for their response, and to any agents who had registered with the MLBPA to receive a copy of the proposed Regulations. The MLBPA requested that all responses be submitted by March 31, 1988, so that the entire process would be completed by Opening Day.

Once the MLBPA received all of the responses, it scheduled a two-day Committee meeting in New York in early May to review everything and finalize the Regulations. By the end of the second day of the meeting, the Committee members had performed some "fine-tuning" of the proposed Regulations, but no drastic changes or additions.

The MLBPA agreed that it would send the finalized proposed Regulations to the Committee members for their review before a final Committee meeting scheduled for June

1, 1988. It also scheduled an Executive Board meeting for June 17th.

The June 1st, the Committee meeting was pretty much a final "rubber stamp" approval. The Committee unanimously recommended that the Executive Board adopt these proposed Regulations as its official MLBPA Regulations Governing Player Agents. The Board did adopt them on June 17, 1988, making that the first day that the Regulations went into effect.

The MLBPA sent copies of the official Regulations to each team, to each of its player members, and to each agent that had registered to receive a copy of the official Regulations. (See the MLBPA's website for a complete copy of the *current* Regulations.)

The MLBPA also announced on that date that it was ready to start implementing the agent certification process as outlined in the Regulations, and that the Application forms to be submitted to start that certification process were now available from the MLBPA.

Ross felt a sense of pride at what the Committee had accomplished in implementing the official Regulations. He was pleasantly surprised to receive from the MLBPA both a plaque and a framed Certificate of Appreciation thanking him for his service as a Committee member. Not bad for a former minor league player with a bum arm.

Even better news was still to come. Wayne Patterson called Ross to tell him that he had just received the Order from the Fifth District Appellate Court of Illinois affirming the jury's entire 5.5-million-dollar award against Sharpe.

They still would have to wait to see whether Sharpe would appeal further to the Illinois Supreme Court. They knew he would with $5.5 million at stake.

The best news came a few months later when the Illinois Supreme Court denied Sharpe's appeal. He would now have to pay the entire $5.5-million award to Lisa. Ross immediately called Lisa, who thanked him repeatedly through her tears.

They both remembered their first encounter after Glenn's death. The award would give Lisa the life that Glenn wanted for her and Ashley.

Ross knew this was what he was meant to be.

ABOUT THE AUTHOR

Steve Trout is a former major league pitcher, primarily for the Chicago White Sox and the Chicago Cubs. A 1976 first-round draft choice of the White Sox, he pitched in the majors from 1978 to 1989. He was represented by the same agents during his entire career, but hired legal representation for fiduciary neglect against those agents. Steve is the only professional baseball player who was a certified player's agent while pitching under contract with the Pittsburgh Pirates. Steve is the co-author of *Home Plate* (2002), the story of the pitching careers of both himself and his father, Paul "Dizzy" Trout as well as *Loosey-Goosey* and *The Magic Ball.* Steve lives in the Chicagoland area and travels the world.